SNOW

THE JEWEL CHRONICLES #2

JEWEL

NATALINA REIS

--------- HOT TREE PUBLISHING ---------

For information, contact the publisher, Hot Tree Publishing.

WWW.HOTTREEPUBLISHING.COM

EDITING: Hot Tree Editing

COVER DESIGNER: Soxsational Cover Art

FORMATTING: RMGraphX

ISBN: 978-1-925655-72-8

MORE FROM NATALINA

*To my mom and dad who exposed me to the world
outside my walls.
Sempre os terei no meu coração.*

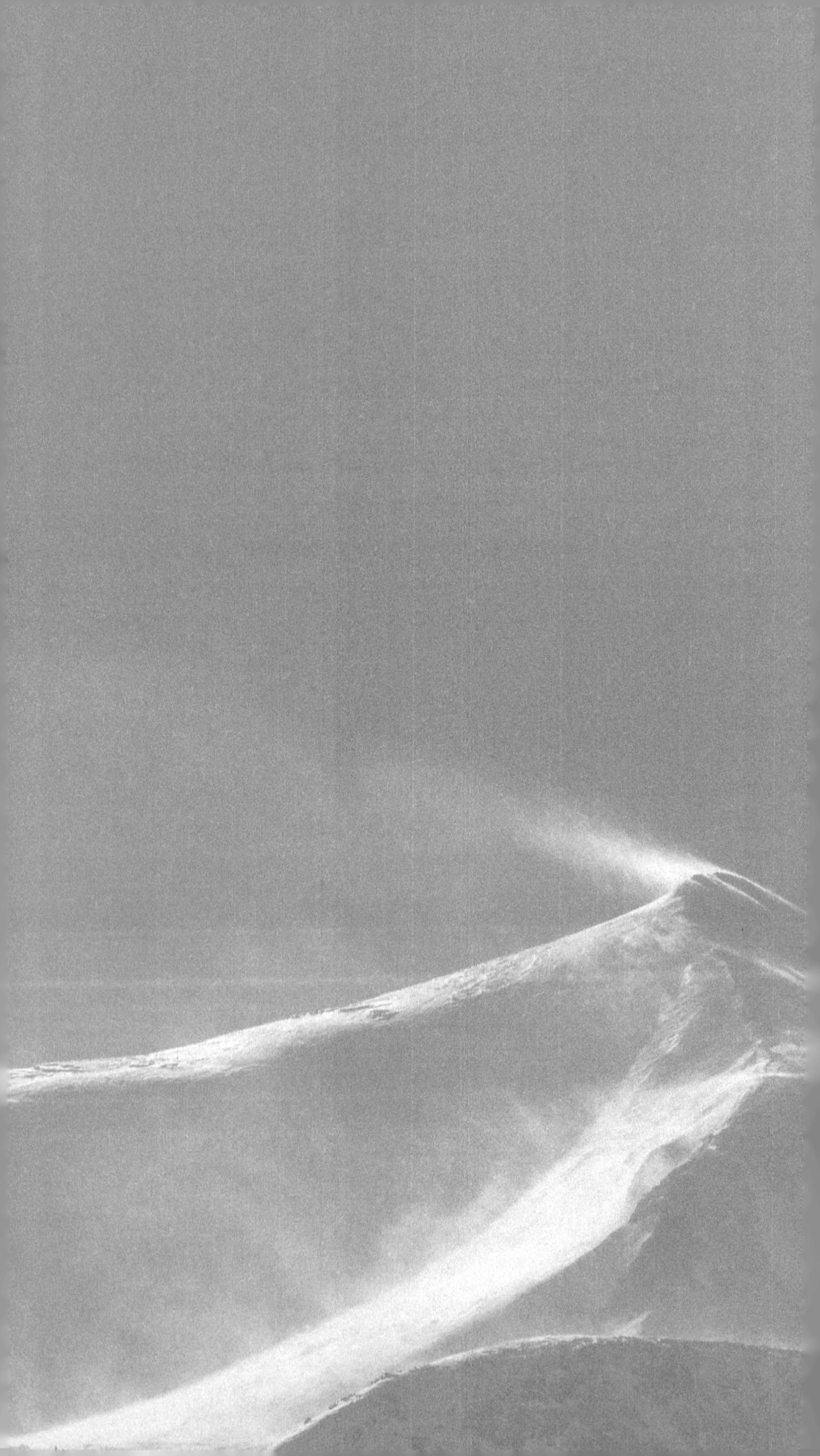

THE JOURNEY

"I know, I know. It's cold, my friend." Mjusi burrowed his nose in the folds of Milenda's *kanga*, whimpering a little. Both their breaths floated up in the air as small clouds to mix and mingle with the white wisps of the early morning fog. The princess, used to the torrid temperatures of Afrika, was having a hard time dealing with the frosty air the northern climate had been showering her with for the past few days. "We're getting closer, Mjusi. Very close."

Milenda was not sure how to feel. A few minutes earlier, as she woke up entangled in Jaali's warm body, she had felt satisfied and excited. They were starting a new life together, free from the constraints and dangers of the Elders' political scheming. Somewhere where she was not the sole heir to the kingdom's throne. Where she was not expected to abide by centuries-old traditions in order to appease the superstitious populace. A place where she would not be expected to change the world. But here, sitting on the cold ship's deck and watching the morning dawn, she felt differently. With each shiver, each shake of her cold body, a kernel of anxiety and sadness sprouted within her heart. Was she doing the right thing by leaving her people in the evil hands of the power-hungry Elders even if only temporarily? Was it morally acceptable to shrug off her responsibilities as the future monarch of Natale to be happy?

The large flying lizard nudged her emphatically, as if he could read her thoughts. "I know it's not all about being happy. I'm protecting my people by vanishing for a while." Mjusi always seemed to know what she was thinking. Growing up together had created a special bond between them that went far beyond that of a pet and its owner. "I wouldn't do them any service by being dead." Which was exactly what would have happened had she stayed in Natale. The Elders had plans that didn't allow for her survival.

It occurred to her that she should get more appropriate clothing now that they had entered the frigid waters of the Northern Sea. Her thin *kanga* dresses and bulky *ibhayi* head coverings did not protect her body from the subzero temperatures of this part of the world. Jaali had told her they would be arriving at the Northern Lands right in the last quarter of the winter season, when the land was covered in snow and ice and only the hardy evergreens stood up to its test. Milenda had never seen snow up close. At certain times of the year, the top of the highest mountains would be dipped in white, but it was so far away it might as well have been the moon. She wondered whether her father had the presence of mind to store warmer clothes in the ship's chests.

The sun was trying to peek through the early morning mist as Milenda and Mjusi were rocked with the rolling of the ocean waves. Several sailors moved about doing what sailors do. Milenda watched them, fascinated as they negotiated the moving floor of the deck with the gracefulness of dancers and hoisted objects three times bigger than them with the ease of jungle apes. What a hard life they must live, always on the go, away from their families, sleeping meager hours in uncomfortable hammocks and cots, and eating the salted and dried stock that could survive such a long trip. A few generations before, these ships would have been obsolete, fodder for museums and history books. But since the big energy depletion a couple hundred years ago, faster vessels and even flying ones had to be kept as backup transportation choices, only to be used on special occasions or in urgent situations.

"You must be freezing." Jaali draped their wedding blanket over her shoulders, and she immediately felt warmer. Covered in his own blanket, he sat next to her. "What are you doing up so early, *msichana*?"

Milenda smiled as she felt her *matangazos*, the cornucopia-shaped grouping of brown spots typical of her people, the Nyotas, heating up along her neck and shoulder at the mere presence of her heart's song. She held his pale hand in hers. He was still warm from the bed, and the ice inside and outside of her melted. "Mjusi and I wanted to see the sunrise, *wimbo wa moyo*. We wanted to know if it was different from Natale's."

"Is it?" Jaali's transparent blue eyes shone in the dusk

as he glanced at her. She still wondered at his out-worldly beauty, the paleness of his skin, the deep lakes of his eyes, and the pearl-like hue of his now longish hair. He was hers and she was his, the *nguba* on her shoulders proof of their union. Husband and wife—it all still sounded unreal, and she was often afraid to wake up and find it had all been a dream.

"We're about to find out." She pointed at the horizon where the sun was finally winning its fight for supremacy over the tendrils of fog. "Glad you're here with me."

With their heads leaning together, they settled on the cold deck to watch the sunrise. Mjusi lifted his head for a moment and looked in the direction of the rising sun, blowing hot air through his massive nostrils before burrowing into Milenda's lap again. She giggled. "I don't think he likes it very much. He's been huffing and puffing since the weather got colder."

"It will get colder still." Jaali patted the *mitzu* before sliding his arm behind her back and closing his hand on her hip. "It's been a long time since I experienced it, but winters are rough up north." His eyes were wistful, as if he wished she would love the snowy north but was afraid she wouldn't. Milenda was happy enough just being alive and safe, so the issue of how much she would like or dislike this new land was a moot point for her. *Isvärld* was her husband's homeland, and she would love it if it was covered in thorns and nettle—which she hoped it wasn't.

The sun stretched and pushed its way through the clouds and fog until it shone sovereign over the ocean and their ship.

However bright, the star didn't have any effect on the biting cold the briny air carried. Milenda shivered against Jaali, and he pulled her closer to him.

"It's beautiful, but maybe we should go inside and warm up." The young Fjorden hopped to his feet and held out his hand to Milenda. "Let's go see if there are any warm clothes on this ship."

The sailors had donned their woolen sweaters and longer pants as soon as the temperatures dipped below the comfortable zone, but Milenda and Jaali had been caught unawares. After all, it wasn't as if they had planned this trip. When King Melchior had them kidnapped and taken to the vessel under the cover of night, he had not shared the plan until they were aboard and in their cabin. Both the princess and her brand-new husband had been caught wearing nothing but their skins in the middle of their wedding night. Believing they had been snatched by minions of the Elders and headed to certain death, they carried with them only a couple blankets to cover themselves with. But surely Milenda's royal father had thought of packing some more suitable clothes.

Their cabin was not big, but it had all the luxuries such a vessel could provide, a comfortable double-wide berth piled high with blankets, and a duvet that had appeared mysteriously out of nowhere a couple nights before. There was a small wooden table and two chairs that, although practical, didn't hold a candle to Jaali's gorgeous wooden furniture. Milenda's heart clenched a bit. Would they ever again see the beautiful art her husband had carved to furnish his humble house? She shook her head and strode to the huge metal chest at the end of their bed just as Mjusi made himself comfortable on the rug. Even after two weeks aboard the slow-moving vessel, she had yet to open the storage chest.

The lid was heavy as it creaked open. "*Wimbo wa moyo*, look!" Inside there were layers upon layers of warm woven cloth, some lined in fur and embroidered with designs she immediately recognized as Fjorden. Much to her surprise, Jaali's expression grew somber at the sight of the exquisite patterns and colors within the chest. "What's wrong?"

"How did Natalians get a hold of so many Fjorden clothes?" His voice was quiet and tinted with a deep sadness. It took Milenda a few moments to understand what he meant. Slaves. Those clothes had been acquired either from the indents brought to Afrika or stolen by the slavers themselves. "These clothes are tainted with pain and loneliness. We can't wear them."

"My father wouldn't be so cruel to send us clothes acquired at the cost of other human lives." *Would he?* At one point, she would not have doubt it, but she had come to know her father better recently, and she wasn't so sure any more. He may be a puppet of the manipulative Elders, but he was not cruel, and he was now, more than ever, cognizant of things he had once chosen to ignore.

Jaali took a step forward and bent down to retrieve a note lying on top of the clothes. As he read it, his expression changed from pained to soft and relaxed. "It's a note from the king. It says these clothes were specially commissioned by him from a group of freed northern slaves for our wedding trousseau." His full lips stretched into a smile, and he glanced at her. "They're brand new and paid for—not stolen."

Milenda jumped to her feet and wrapped her brown arms around her groom, a giggle escaping her lips. She was relieved to find out her father was indeed a good man. Seeing Jaali's smile made her heart sing. "I knew it! I knew he would never do that."

Their lips met, and her *matangazos* shone as brightly as the sun in the sky, making her skin tingle and burn pleasantly. Jaali brushed his fingers across her neck and shoulder, tracing the glowing markings in her skin, and kissed her again. "I love you, *msichana*."

Milenda sighed deeply into his mouth and allowed her body to go soft in his arms. She loved the way he tasted, a mixture of sweetness and tartness that reminded her of the iced treats she had grown up eating. "I love you too, *wimbo wa moyo*." She would never tire of his kiss, of his touch. No matter how far they must go, how long they must run. They were one forever.

* * *

MILENDA

"He *is* handsome—for a mortal." The voice made her sit up so quickly, stars swam in her eyes. "You'll wake him up, Jewel." Yemanjá sat on the edge of Milenda's bed, beautiful and formidable as only a demigoddess could be, tsking and glaring at her. "You sure are jumpy for someone who just defied the rulers of her own nation."

Milenda glanced at Jaali, the image of bliss as he slept by her side, his now longer hair splayed on the pillow around his head like a halo. He didn't stir, his quiet breathing reaching her ears with the softness of feathers. What was she doing here? In a ship in the middle of an ocean? "Yemanjá, what brings you here?"

The beautiful black woman smiled, her lips stretching from ear to ear and her brown eyes glittering in the dimness of the cabin. "You mean to ask me, how come I can visit you here so far from my realm, right?" Milenda had to smile. There was no point in trying to hide her surprise from Yemanjá. "Well, the gods' world is complex and entwined in some ways. I put in a special request to my equal in these parts."

Gods had equals? And they actually talked to each other? "May I ask who?" Milenda was curious, still learning as she was about the unseen world of the deities working their magic in this world.

"Freya. She's more than glad to help out another female fight the patriarchs of this earth." A giggle escaped the princess's lips. Goddesses had to fight for their rights as well? Maybe things were not that different between the world of the mortals and that of the powers that be. "As soon as she gave me permission, I projected myself here so I could talk to you." Then again, maybe things were very different indeed.

"How's Mama Nyeusi?" Milenda's *iyalorixá* had stayed behind in Afrika with the promise to keep an eye on her father, but the princess missed the closest thing she had to a mother. Her eyes blurred with tears at the thought of being away from her *iyalorixá* for a long time.

"Child, you worry about the unnecessary." Yemanjá waved a dismissive hand in front of her face. "But if you must know she is doing fine. She's taking care of a little issue for me while you're gone."

That piqued Milenda's curiosity. "Oh yes? What could that be? Nothing dangerous, I hope." Mama Nyeusi was not a young woman anymore.

"That old kook is a lot tougher than you give her credit for." The demigoddess leaned toward Milenda and placed a cold hand on hers. Milenda flinched. The deity had never touched her before, except for the time she had placed her hand on Milenda's *matangazos*. Because of that touch, Milenda was now in possession of a special power that still wowed and scared her. She could project herself—not unlike Yemanjá—to wherever Jaali was, no matter how far. The Mother seemed to have guessed her fears. "I'm not gifting you with any special gifts, child. Just touching at the request of your *iyalorixá*. Superstitious woman that she is, she wanted me to touch you for protection."

Milenda's eyes widened. "It doesn't work that way?" Popular belief had it that the touch of the Mother was the most powerful protection of all.

"Well, maybe a little." Yemanjá giggled, her crystalline laughter echoing through the cabin and yet not waking up Jaali. Was he not able to hear her? "No, he can't hear me.

There are perks to being a demigoddess, you know." She laughed again, amused by her own joke. "You have both my protection and that of Freya as long as you make her proud."

Making Freya proud? How? She knew nothing about this goddess of the North. "How can I do that? I'm not one of her children."

"Don't be so obtuse, Jewel. You're the hope of a whole nation." That again. Even here, thousands of miles away from her own home, she couldn't escape the burden of her birth. "You're also the one who freed a son of Freya."

"Jaali had been free for many years before we met, Mother." It was true. Jaali had achieved his freedom from slavery years before they crashed into each other that rainy day at the university. Milenda smiled at the memory; her hair dripping, her slippers soaked, her books being rescued from the puddles by a white-haired, ethereal young scholar. He had looked so beautiful to her, standing there amid an awful downpour.

The *orisa*'s expression softened then. "But you did, my sweet Jewel. He was not truly free from what had been done to him until you killed his demons with your love. Freya is well aware of that. She also knows you will fight to end the flow of slavers who come to her land and steal her children."

Jaali had freed her too. From the loneliness and isolation she lived with every day because of her royal station. He had freed her from the fear of rising against those who would keep her people in ignorance for their own political and financial purposes. And he had freed her from a lifetime in a loveless marriage.

"So, I must thank her and hope I will be worthy of her faith in me." It had always been hard for her to be subservient, even to the gods, but under Mama Nyeusi tutelage she had learned to make herself humble when required or expected.

Yemanjá laughed yet again. "Jewel, meekness doesn't suit you. But thank you for trying." Her hand, now removed, had left a strange cooling sensation on her skin as that of mint leaves on your tongue. "Your old *iyalorixá* is making sure to put a few drops of a certain oil in your father's soon-to-be-wife's tea every day before she goes to bed."

Milenda was horrified. "You're making Mama Nyeusi poison my father's new bride?" The princess didn't even know this woman who was to be her new stepmother or cared for her. She knew all too well that her only purpose was to give the kingdom a new heir and make Milenda's life a lot less indispensable. Yet, killing this innocent woman was not the right thing to do.

"Now you're being plain daft." The *orisa*'s eyes hardened. "Of course I wouldn't have her killed. She hasn't done anything wrong. The oil is a contraceptive. We're just making sure she does not conceive any time soon."

Milenda sighed in relief. "Will it prevent her from ever having children?" That would be cruel as well. In a world where fertile males were at a premium, not being able to procreate was unfair to the whole nation.

"The effect lasts only while she's taking it. That's why it's important she drinks that tea every night." Yemanjá stood up. She smoothed out the creases in her golden *kanga* and straightened the *gele* on her head. "I better go. This cold air does not agree with me a bit. I don't know how Freya does it."

Mjusi, who had been fast asleep through the whole exchange, lifted his green scaly head and snorted, little puffs of mist coming out of his nose. Was he getting sick? "Do you think Mjusi caught something? He's doing that a lot."

Yemanjá threw a glance at the large reptile and cooed. "He's just coming in to his own, that's all. He'll be fine." Cryptic as usual, she wavered for a second or two, and vanished. Milenda had no idea what she meant, but at least she knew that both her father and Mama Nyeusi were doing well.

Beside her, Jaali stirred. "Are you all right, *msichana*?" His hand automatically sought her body, and she reclined onto the pillow, cherishing the feeling of his warm hand on her belly. "I thought I heard voices."

Should she tell him about Yemanjá's visit? He knew about her and how she had been instrumental in helping him through the Trials in the desert. But his hand slid up to her breast, making her burst into flames. She would tell him later. After the languid kiss that tasted like ambrosia and melted her inside. After she enjoyed his lips and his fingers exploring her body. Much, much later after he took her up into cloud nine again from where the earth and life in general seemed tiny and insignificant. Yes, she would tell him later.

ISVÄRLD

JAALI

The activity on the deck had taken a turn to a frenzy of men running from one side of the ship to another, climbing masts, and yelling out things and names Jaali could not make sense of. Dressed in the warm clothes they had found in their cabin, he and Milenda had come up onto the deck to check on what was happening. They were not ready for what awaited at a distance in the calm waters of the Northern Sea—a landscape that was as beautiful as it was austere. A dark gray cliff stretched to the blue skies above, spotted here and there with the white paint of snow and ice. On the bottom, nestled among more rocks, tiny specks of red and white stood witness to the presence of other humans.

The wind of the past few days had calmed, and the ocean waves had finally subsided into gentle rolls. Milenda burrowed deeper into the shelter of Jaali's arms, never once taking her eyes off the scenery. "Is that *Isvärld,* Jaali?" Mjusi had wobbled up to the deck after them and was now flapping his wings, as if trying to take off.

Jaali sighed. It had been so long since he had seen his native land, he couldn't quite tell. "I don't know. I was just a child when I left. It could be." He tightened his hold on her. "I do remember the cliffs and the small red houses."

Mjusi frantically moved his wings and grunted. "It's beautiful." Milenda stared at the great lizard who was now scratching his talons on the deck and throwing his head backward. "What do you think he's doing?"

With a chuckle, Jaali called the *msitu*. Mjusi twisted his neck to stare at the two of them for a moment and then resumed his strange behavior. "Who knows? It's not like we know much about his kind. Maybe he's excited about seeing land finally." It had been a long trip, stuck on a small ship for weeks, enduring the angry waters and eating the less-than-appetizing food aboard. Who could blame the flying creature for being excited about the smell of land?

Now that the shore was approaching swiftly, Milenda had become more animated, almost jittery. Jaali wondered whether she was thinking of what she had left behind. Her life in Natale was far from perfect, and being royalty didn't afford her many friends, but she had her father with whom she had recently become closer. And there was Mama Nyeusi who was the closest thing she had to a mother. The weather in Natale was so extremely opposite to that of *Isvärld*, the two nations might as well be on different planets. Jaali remembered how he felt those first few months after his kidnapping. Not only had he been scared out of his wits, but it had been difficult to adapt to the dry—or sometimes extremely humid—heat of Afrika, being accustomed to the icy cold embrace of the northern climates.

"How are you feeling?" Even though the idea of coming back home was exciting, it was also scary. He had grown up in Natale and been an obvious foreigner who stuck out from the rest of the population, but Jaali loved Afrika. His memories of his family were blurry, and he often wondered whether they were true memories or something his heart had made up to compensate for the lack of love in his life. He didn't want Milenda to feel that way. "Are you missing home already?"

Milenda smiled, her *matangazos* visible even through her thick coat as she cuddled against him further. "Not yet. A little nervous, but excited. I want to know where you came from. I want to meet your family and learn your traditions. Maybe Yemanjá wanted to give us this—a moment of being just the two of us, getting to know each other better." He doubted that, romantic an idea as it was. The demigoddess was purely trying to protect the crown princess from certain death. He did not know why, but the gods seemed to favor the two of them. It made him anxious. Gods were often selfish and numb to human feelings and problems. For them to be so invested in Milenda's future could mean a lot of trouble for both of them.

The giant cliff approached, and as it got closer, they could discern many small houses, poppies with black roofs peppering the white-stained rocks on the shore. Just when it seemed the ship would crash into it, the vessel veered off to the right and went around the big cliff. On the other side, there hid a natural harbor framed by small islands covered in snow. A tiny village took residence on these islands and peninsulas, with homes built around a central lighthouse. They had arrived.

"We'll be dropping anchor in a few minutes." The captain was a big man, brown face weathered by the ocean's salty air and the strong rays of the sun, with strong muscles that bulged from underneath his thick clothes. "We will have to take the dinghy ashore. Make sure you have all your gear ready for the men to bring it up."

Milenda called to Mjusi who paced the deck, waving his long, thick tail around, often hitting the sailors' legs and causing a litany of curses. "He's acting so strangely."

The three went down to their cabin to pack the few items they had brought with them. Jaali made sure to pack the *nguba* safely inside the big chest, along with a few of the books King Melchior had been kind enough to include with the winter clothes. Now that they were here, Jaali's mind and heart were filled to the brim with questions and doubts. What if he had no family left? Or if they had all gone somewhere else? How had they fared all these years since he had been taken? He couldn't help but be nervous. It had been over fifteen years since he had set foot on *Isvärld*.

Packed together with their luggage and an agitated Mjusi into a small dinghy, Jaali and Milenda watched the approaching shore with interest. The chill of the arctic air made the young Fjorden shiver. His body no longer accepted the cold as natural, it seemed. Despite everything, he smiled, amused and sad at the same time. He didn't belong anywhere anymore. No matter where he was, he would always be an outsider.

Once they hit the shore, two of the sailors jumped out and held the small vessel so they could disembark with no incidents. Two other men carried the large trunk with their luggage onto the solid rock that formed the seaboard and led the way in the direction of the red roof building a few hundred feet away from them. The captain had joined them in their excursion ashore, no doubt following orders from the monarch who employed him. Jaali wondered how the king had ensured these men wouldn't tell the Elders about their escape. Maybe Melchior still had some faithful followers, or maybe they owed the monarch a favor. He only hoped the king's faith in their silence was not misplaced.

"Captain Kifeda, how far can you take us?" Milenda voiced the question Jaali had in his mind.

The weathered man didn't take his eyes from the rocky terrain. "As far as that house." Jaali gasped in surprise. They were going to leave them there? In a place they were not even sure where it was? "That's a mercantile outpost. Fjordens don't trust Natalians, but they need a lot of our goods. This is about the only place in the whole nation that will sell us the supplies we need for our trip back home. We can't go further inland without running the risk of being imprisoned." Not surprising, considering the Mabaya warriors had been kidnapping Fjorden children for generations.

"But we don't know where to go. Or how to get there." Milenda's voice had an edge of panic to it. Jaali pressed her against his side. "Jaali was a child when he was taken away.

He can't possibly remember the way."

The captain stared stubbornly at the ground and kept walking, his step long and steady. "They will help you at the outpost. They will welcome him as one of their own. Different from us." What did that mean for Milenda? She was a Natalian, her dark skin even now in vivid contrast with the whiteness of the snow and her winter clothes. Would they welcome her as his wife? Or would they shun her as the enemy? Jaali had never considered the reactions of a nation who undoubtedly felt a seething hate for the people who had stolen many of their children.

Milenda tugged at Jaali's arm as her step became heavier and slower. Mjusi, as if feeling the change in her mood, stopped his flight ahead and came to walk beside them, whimpering in sympathy. "What if they hate me?" His stomach plummeted as her words reflected his own doubts. "What if they look at me and see a Mabaya warrior, a child thief, a slaver?"

It was too late now for second thoughts. They either stayed and faced the possible disapproval and dislike of Jaali's own people or they returned to Afrika and faced certain death. Neither of the choices were good, but one had at least a chance of survival. They would stay and face whatever was waiting for them and make the best of it.

As soon as the men in front of them opened the door to the squat building, a wave of warm air broke over their bodies. The soothing air enveloped them in a sense of comfort they hadn't felt since the ship had entered the cold climate of the far north. Jaali and Milenda ducked under the low doorway and into the warmth of the outpost. It was a small place but packed to the ceiling with supplies of every kind. Right away, Jaali saw boxes of dried foods, clothing, tools, blankets, and even weapons stacked in giant piles against the walls. On the far wall, facing the door, there was a long wooden counter. A tall man, with hair the same color as Jaali's, was behind it. At the sound of the opening door, he looked up and frowned.

"Hey there, Karlsson," the captain called, waving his hand. "Long time no see." The blond man smiled then and walked around the counter to greet the captain with an effusive handshake. "I bring you some travelers."

The captain pointed at a nervous Jaali and his princess standing slightly behind him. Karlsson squinted at the couple. "*For søren*! A Fjorden!" He dropped the captain's hand and advanced quickly toward Jaali who cringed in surprise. Grabbing hold of his hand, the man shook it enthusiastically. "Were you taken?"

Jaali blushed. No matter how many years had passed, he still felt the familiar pang of pain anytime he thought or spoke of his kidnapping. "Yes, over fifteen years ago. Jaali Asker from Örebro." His hand went slack within the man's own, suddenly afraid of hearing bad news about his family. "Do you know them?"

The man's full lips stretched into a friendly smile. "Yes, I know them. They came here often, years ago, to inquire about you. Many families came looking for their little ones." His eyes strayed to Milenda, who still held on to her husband's arm as if her life depended on it. His smile turned into a frown, and his eyes froze over. "What is she doing here?"

Jaali dropped the man's hand and turned to Milenda. "This is my wife, Milenda."

Karlsson's jaw dropped. "Your wife? You're married to one of them?" The look he gave Milenda was not unfriendly, but it also lacked any warmth.

"What do you mean, one of them?" Jaali bristled at the man's tone of voice, something in between disbelief and amusement.

"One of the Afrikans." The man didn't flinch. It was puzzling to Jaali that he could talk like that in front of the captain, who not only was an Afrikan as well, but seemed to be on friendly terms with the merchant. "You do realize that they have been stealing our children for over two centuries, right? You are one of those children. How could you marry one of them?"

Milenda's hand tightened on his arm, as if she was afraid he would do something he would regret. "You are speaking of the Mabaya warriors. My wife is not one of them. And for your information, sir, Milenda is one of the many Natalians fighting to put an end to such trafficking."

The merchant raised his hands in front of him and shook his head. "Hey, no skin off my nose. I'm just a businessman. But when you bring her into town, you better be prepared for a strong reaction. For generations, the Mabaya warriors, like you call them, have been sneaking onto our lands at night and spiriting our children away. The parents' pain has blinded them to everything else but the color of the traffickers' skin."

Milenda trembled against Jaali, the reality of their situation suddenly sinking in for both of them. The princess wouldn't be welcomed. If he had been gawked at and had to endure the whispers and curiosity of the native Natalians, she would have to face something even worse—the anger of a whole civilization of people who needed to blame someone for the evils done to them throughout the years.

"I'm sure my family will accept her and love her once they realize the goodness in her heart." Not sure whether he was saying it to appease Milenda's obvious fears or his own, Jaali squeezed her hand in his and smiled at her. "Milenda is more than my wife. She is my savior." Pulling her closer to him, he planted a kiss on her forehead.

The man hooked both thumbs into the belt loops on his pants and spread his legs apart. "I don't get into politics, so you and your wife will always be welcomed here. I just wanted to warn you."

The captain, who had just returned from aiding the other sailors pick supplies, looked at the three of them. "Karlsson, can you put them up for the night? It will be dark soon, and they don't know the roads well."

"Sure, I have a couple rooms available in the inn. Tomorrow I will have one of my boys drive you into town."

The man barked something Jaali couldn't understand, and less than a minute later, a young woman emerged from a door to the side of the counter. The girl—for she couldn't be more than sixteen or seventeen—had golden hair that fell over her shoulders in two long braids. She wore a colorful embroidered vest over a plain white shirt and a red skirt that ballooned around her stockinged shins. Pretty fur-lined black boots completed her outfit.

"*Ja, papa? Vad vill du?*" Jaali understood that. She wanted to know why her father had called her there. He sighed in relief. For a moment, he had thought he had lost his knowledge of his native language. Karlsson must also speak a dialect he was not familiar with. The girl stopped in her tracks when she noticed the beautiful but different young woman in the store. "What is this *smsitugt tjuv* doing here?" Jaali recognized the words for filthy thief and immediately stepped forward to protest. Milenda stopped him again.

"Watch your mouth, *litet barn*. These are guests, and you will be respectful to them both. Understood?" Karlsson's voice left no room for discussion, and in spite of his earlier feelings, Jaali felt his heart beginning to warm up toward the short merchant. "This is Jaali Asker from Örebro and his wife, Milenda…?"

"Nwosu." It was Milenda who finished the sentence, her hand grabbing the edges of her furry hood and pulling it backward to reveal her full head of wild dark curls and kinks. "Milenda Nwosu. Very grateful and honored for your hospitality. *Trevligt att träffas.*" Jaali's chest almost puffed out in pride, hearing his bride greet the father and daughter in his native language. He had spent a lot of time teaching Milenda his language on the long voyage here.

The young girl stole a glance at her father, and then, lowering her head, gave Milenda a short curtsy. "Welcome to our home, honored guests." The formal memorized words came out easily even if her lips were set in a thin line that belied them.

"Alva, take them to the blue room and prepare them a meal." Karlsson turned to them as soon as his daughter left the room. "I suggest you eat in your room and make yourselves scarce. We have quite a few people from town here tonight. Some came looking for their children who disappeared while they slept a week ago."

"I'm ashamed that those horrible traffickers are my people." Although loud and clear, Milenda's voice shook. Her whole body trembled in anger. Jaali had seen it before when he'd revealed what had been done to him as a young man in his teens. "I have no way of making it up to you and your people, but you have my word that as soon as I can, this unspeakable practice will be put to an end."

Karlsson twisted one of the edges of his mustache. "I appreciate you saying that, and I believe you mean well, but who are you to change something that's been a fact of our lives since we were born? You're nothing but a young woman, barely weened of your mother's breast."

Jaali knew she was not quite as powerless as she looked. Not in theory anyway. He also knew that the day Milenda was allowed to go back to Afrika, she would fight with every fiber of her tiny body to end slavery. Why else would the Elders be so obsessed with getting rid of her? They too knew that they had a formidable opponent in the princess. He held her back. It wouldn't be wise to divulge her title to anyone at this point. Not yet. Not until they were sure the information wouldn't go straight back to the Elders who thought them dead.

"We thank you, Herr Karlsson. *Tack så mycket.*" Jaali pulled Milenda against him again, preventing her from protesting the man's words. "But we are very tired, and if you don't mind, we would like to retire to our room."

They hastily said their goodbyes, for the sailors seemed anxious to leave the outpost for the relative safety of the ship, and soon they were alone in the so-called blue room. As it turned out, it was an appropriate name for it because most of the decor, including the color of the walls, were in different shades of blue. It was a simple room, with a free-standing bed tucked into a wall, a tiny window covered with lace curtains, and a square wooden table and two chairs. The bed was piled high with white and blue duvets. A fire had been lit in the corner hearth, the flames emitting soothing warm air into the space.

They stood by the closed door for a few moments, studying the room, taking in the strangeness of the environment. It felt foreign even for him, who had been born in this land. For a second, Jaali missed his old *hema* with the artisanal furniture he had carved and shaped out of wood and Milenda loved so much. But here they would be safe. Milenda would be safe. Or would she?

***

MILENDA

The *msitu* growled, a quiet rumble coming from deep within

his green chest as he paced, circling around as if following his own tail in the same spot. Milenda was worried about him. Mjusi seemed agitated and quite unlike himself ever since they had spotted land. Even though they had a close connection, they couldn't talk to each other, and she felt helpless not knowing exactly what was bothering her scaly friend. Before he left to go to the communal baths, Jaali had placed a large pile of blankets by the hearth so the flying lizard would have a comfortable, warm place to sleep. But he wouldn't rest. One minute he was lying down, his tail curled up to his nose, the next he was pacing around again, doing that funny little sound within his throat that eerily resembled a human moan.

"I'm not too crazy about this place either, my friend." Tired of watching the creature pace around, Milenda sat next to it on the piled-up bedding and slid a hand over his back. "I don't think we will be welcomed the way we thought we would. But then again, why would I expect a different reaction? My people have proven to be untrustworthy and cruel to the Fjorden." Mjusi growled again. "Are you sick? What's wrong? I want to help, but I don't know how."

The flying reptile laid his nose on Milenda's lap and, with a little whimper, fell asleep. The princess brushed her hands across his back and his head, the spikes on his neck tickling the palms of her hands as they grazed her skin. Mjusi had been her friend since she was a toddler. She couldn't bear seeing him unwell—even though she was not sure that's what was happening. His action denoted more of anxiety rather than pain or discomfort of any kind.

The young blonde girl had brought them a delicious stew of some kind of meat in wooden bowls Milenda recognized as twins to those Jaali had in his *hema* back in Natale. In spite of all the heartache the past few months had brought upon them, a wave of nostalgia came over her. She missed Mama Nyeusi, Jaali's and her secret meeting place in the forest, and the university where she had met her husband on a rainy day. She had hoped for a warm welcome from Jaali's people. She had hoped that, lost in the joy of seeing him again, they would ignore the fact that her skin color matched his kidnappers'. As it turned out, it was starting to feel as if they had jumped from the fire into the cauldron of a wakening volcano.

With care, Milenda covered the *msitu* and crawled in bed, huddling under the mountain of duvets and blankets. She was exhausted. Life on the ship was not private or restful. The vessel rocked hard most of the time, leaving her nauseous and achy. Now that they were finally back ashore, her legs felt gelatinous and weak, as if the floor beneath them was still rocking back and forth.

Sleep overtook her quicker than she thought possible, and she dreamed of her homeland. The dream was so vivid, she could feel the heat of the Afrikan sun kiss her face. With a start, she realized it was not a dream. Jaali had quietly slid into bed with her and the heat of the sun was coming from his lips.

Milenda swept her fingers through his long, silvery hair and sighed. How could she truly regret being here? She had done it for love. Love for her husband and her people.

One day soon they would return to the tropical climates of Natale and make things right. In the meantime, she was here with Jaali, the man with the sky in his eyes, those pale blue eyes that made her melt inside and out. Her lips sought his with a hunger that surprised even her. He yielded to her insistent tongue, letting her in to savor him fully. Milenda would never get tired of his taste, the way he felt against her, the way he filled her.

"I love you, *wimbo wa moyo*." His warm hands skimmed her waist, under the thin linen of her nightgown, and gently tugged on the garment, pulling it up over her head. She felt the skin of her breasts pucker in reaction to his hand grazing against them. Jaali was naked and swollen with desire. A shiver of pleasure ran through her. It still awed her to think anyone would feel like that about her. Then again, all it took was a touch of his hand to turn her into liquid.

"I love you too, *msichana*." As if to prove his words to be true, the Fjorden lowered his mouth to her breast and took it between his lips. Milenda arched against him, in a mixture of pleasure and agony, the pleasing feel of his tongue sliding over her sensitive skin and the agony of wanting more.

She wrapped her legs around his waist and quivered as her heat mingled with his. She needed him inside her, physically and spiritually, not allowing any space for doubt or fear. "Take me, Jaali. Please."

Jaali flipped her around and lowered her onto him, the length of him exciting and soothing all at once as it filled her fully. She moaned, her head lolling forward against his. She moved then, in an ironic mimicry of the movement of their ship, rocking back and forth as Jaali moaned softly until they came together in ecstasy.

Sleep took them in its gentle arms, their bodies wrapped in each other's and hearts beating in unison. Tomorrow the next leg of their journey—and possibly the hardest—would start, but for the moment, they were happy and relaxed in the knowledge their love for each other would carry them through whatever awaited ahead.

ARRIVAL

MILENDA

The silence of the morning lay over the outpost like a blanket of soft cotton, bestowing the place with a layer of otherworldly tranquility. Milenda stretched, supporting herself on her tiptoes and yawning quietly by the small window in the room. The snowy landscape seemed to go on forever, the whiteness spreading as far as the eye could see in thousands of tiny rounded mounds that reminded her of Afrikan ant hills. It was beautiful and peaceful. A kind of quiet beauty unlike anything she had ever seen or experienced. The lush jungles of her nation were peaceful but never quiet. Even at night, the insects and nocturnal animals hooted and creaked in a cacophony of sounds, reassuring but noisy. Jaali's ice paradise was in a totally different league.

Milenda rested her forehead on the cold window and sighed. Maybe things wouldn't be as bad as they seemed. There was a chance—however small—that Jaali's people would accept her for who she was—the woman who loved the silver-haired Fjorden more than life itself. Deep down inside, she doubted it though. Hate was a sentiment hard to eradicate from your heart. And Fjordens had a lot of good reasons to hate her kind.

"Wait until you see the northern lights." Jaali had come from behind, silent on bare feet, and wrapped his arms around her waist, resting his chin on her shoulder. Milenda felt immediately soothed and turned her face to lightly kiss the corner of his mouth. "When the night sky lights up with the wavering lights of the midnight sun, it's almost as if looking into another world."

"Midnight sun? Is that a real thing?" She wiggled in place, so her back would fit better with the curve of his body leaning against her. The sun had not fully risen, still peeking shyly from behind the white horizon and painting the snow in a rainbow of oranges and reds, the same colors of the Afrikan sun at the crack of dawn.

Jaali laughed softly. "Not really. That's just what we call it." He tightened his hold on her, turning his face to kiss the sensitive spot behind her ear. "The scientists call it a collision of particles. When the particles of the sun meet those of our atmosphere, it creates this amazing display of lights. It's pretty romantic actually."

It was Milenda's turn to laugh. "Romantic? Particles crashing into each other? A bit too scientific to be romantic, don't you think?" At the university in Natale, Milenda had never found the time to take science classes, other than the basic ones. Science fascinated her, but not as much as art.

She'd chosen art instead.

The Fjorden's hand starfished across her stomach, the heat of his palm making Milenda shiver in delight. From the corner of her eye, she could see the soft glare of her *matangazos* reacting to his touch.

"Think about it." His soft, melodious voice blew a gust of warm air into her ear. "These particles are floating around in space, lonely and lost until they find their polar opposites. Their joining is so overwhelmingly pleasurable and fulfilling that they explode in a colorful firework of lights across the sky."

Her breathing became shallow as Jaali's words reached her senses with the same effect of an intimate caress. "Kind of like us...." Jaali turned her within the circle of his arms and lowered his lips onto hers. Yes, a lot like them. Milenda could see the flashes of brilliant, colorful lights from beneath her closed eyelids as her *wimbo wa moyo* explored her mouth with his tongue and his hand cupped the back of her neck, supporting her trembling body.

A kiss led to another and yet another, her body craving her husband's, but knowing all too well time was not on their side. Reluctantly she pulled herself apart from Jaali with a sigh. It was time to get ready to go. After a perfunctory wash, they put on layer after layer of fur-lined woolen items. By the time they were ready, they were both so covered by clothing, there was no danger of either of them being recognized. Milenda's dark skin was buried beneath layers of fabric, gloves, and even a balaclava that effectively covered her whole face.

Milenda laughed, the sound muffled by the woolen knit of the face covering. "I think we may have found the solution to all our problems. I can just walk around in this contraption every time I'm in public." Her body, used to being covered in only a layer of thin cotton or silk, was itchy and uncomfortable, but she knew it to be necessary for the climate they were to face on their way to Örebro.

Herr Karlsson was waiting for them by the front door, hot coffee in hand and a plate of hot bread and butter. "You must eat before facing the cold out there. The sleigh is ready for you out back."

Milenda had no idea what a sleigh was, but she was hungry, and the hot bread was delicious as she washed it down with the comforting warmth of the coffee. She had a new favorite food, and *Isvärld* was looking better by the time she finished licking the creamy sweet butter off her fingers.

Karlsson led them to the back. "I'm sorry I couldn't be more welcoming," he said, his hand waving up in the air. "I understand you have nothing to do with the kidnappings, but I never had any children or siblings taken away from their bed in the dark of the night like others have. I wish you all the luck, and you can call on me if you ever need something I can help you with. But I can't change people's minds."

Milenda knew that all too well. Even as a princess, she had not been able to change her own people's minds into sparing her hopefuls from the cruelty of the Trials. The same Trials that had nearly killed Jaali.

The princess wanted to hug the stocky man. Or shake his hand. Something to assure him she didn't blame him and that she was grateful for his hospitality. But she was not sure what was acceptable in this culture, what was viewed as socially appropriate. So she didn't do anything.

"You're sure you don't need my son to drive you there?" Karlsson asked Jaali.

"He told me to follow the road posts, and as long as I keep to the road, I'll be fine." Jaali had had a long conversation with the young man the night before. "We don't want to inconvenience you any more than we already have. But thank you for the offer."

They had arrived at the back door, and a gust of icy cold wind hit them with the strength of a punch as Karlsson opened it to reveal a horse-pulled contraption Milenda could only guess was the aforementioned sleigh.

"What beautiful creatures." In awe of the horses, tawny and thick haired with a pure white spot on their heads, Milenda stepped forward, her hand stretched out toward the creatures. The horses neighed and shook their abundant manes, flicking snow all over the her. Milenda laughed, delighted. "Spunky creatures, aren't you?"

Mjusi growled, either annoyed by all the fooling around or jealous his human friend was paying attention to the strange creatures instead of him. Milenda turned and motioned him closer. "Come here, my friend. Come and look at these amazing animals. They're beautiful, aren't they, Mjusi?" The *msitu* moved his head up and down, as if agreeing, and nuzzled one of the horses. "Look, they like you."

Karlsson's mouth was wide open. "What is that creature?" The winged reptile had sneaked in their room through the window last night, skittish about the strange pale humans in the store. Now both the outpost owner and his daughter seemed almost scared of the flying lizard making friends with their horses. Mjusi hissed at them, flapping his great wings and blowing mist through his wide nostrils. "*For søren*! It's a dragon." The man took two steps backward, almost tripping over Jaali.

Milenda laughed. "It's a *msitu*, a flying jungle lizard." Mjusi, obviously gratified with the reaction he warranted from the pale humans, hissed louder and shook his massive tail, nearly hitting the horse's legs. "He's my best friend."

Karlsson's eyes bulged out, and his daughter ran to hide inside. "Dragons are dangerous and haven't been seen in these parts for centuries." The man looked ready to throw up or bolt down the snow-covered path.

"No, no. I assure you that Mjusi is harmless." Jaali took a step forward, bringing his hand down on the man's shoulder. "He wouldn't hurt a fly, I swear."

The man relaxed a little, but he seemed to be in a rush to get rid of them all of a sudden. He helped Milenda up on the red sleigh, a device that looked a bit like the oxen-pulled carts of Natale but moved on large, long blades instead of wheels. Milenda admired the woodwork and was reminded of what Jaali had told her months ago—that Fjorden slaves were sought after by the Mabaya warriors because of their skills as carpenters. A wave of familiar guilt rose to her cheeks, and her *matangazos* burned with anger underneath all the layers of clothing. Being the future monarch of a nation that still condoned slavery in any form brought her searing shame. It didn't matter that she intended to change that once on the throne; knowing that her family line had never tried to stop such an ignoble practice was almost too much to bear.

Jaali jumped in after placing their one heavy trunk in the back of the sleigh. He pulled the furry blanket Herr Karlsson had left in the vehicle over their legs and motioned Mjusi to join them. The flying creature hissed at Karlsson one last time and, with a big flap of wings, flew the short space up to the sled and curled up with a sigh of satisfaction by their feet.

"Are you sure you remember how to drive one of these?" Milenda looked at the horses, clutching the blanket on her lap and shifting in her seat.

"I guess we're about to find out." With a last wave to the outpost owner, Jaali snapped the reins gently, and the princess let out a gasp of delight as the horses began to move forward. "So far so good, *msichana.*"

Soon the red building was nothing but a dot in the horizon as they made their way along the snow-covered road, the horses in no hurry to get to Örebro it seemed. Milenda didn't mind. She was now so afraid of what Jaali's people's reaction to her would be that her neck and shoulder constantly stung along her *matangazos.* With her arm hooked around Jaali's, she rested her hooded head on his shoulder, cursing the layers of fabric that separated their bodies. Milenda wanted to make her *matangazos* burn with pleasure, not with anxiety and fear.

"Are you worried?" Jaali's voice was muffled by the knitted balaclava covering his face, but she could see the anxiety reflected in his transparent eyes.

She wouldn't lie. Not to her love. "Yes, I'm afraid they'll hate me because of where I come from." And she so wanted Jaali's family to love her. "It's not like I can hide the color of my skin. What if they hate you because you love me?"

A cloud of anger shadowed the lakes of his eyes. "Let them hate me then. Of everything that I ever did or happened in my life, you're the one thing I will never regret. You saved me, *msichana*. You slayed all my demons and gave me what I never thought I'd have—happiness and love."

Milenda was silent for a while, hanging firmly on to Jaali's arms. Once in a while, the sleigh would slide over some bump on the road and her body was thrown against her husband's, but the ride had been surprisingly smooth and uneventful. There was nothing to see other than snow and the sporadic tree along the road. They passed what Milenda thought was a frozen lake, the blue of the waters now white and glassy, glittering in the glare of the sun.

"It must have been so difficult." Her voice startled Jaali into moving his eyes from the road ahead to stare at her in confusion. "To live among those who enslaved you and be so… visible. Like me, you couldn't hide the color of your skin, the one thing that marked you as an outsider, an outcast. I can't imagine how hard it must have been to want to hide and yet be seen all the time."

"I admit, it was difficult." Jaali returned his eyes to the road. "Sometimes more than others. But it was all worth it because I found you." He laughed. "Well, I crashed into you to be more precise." Milenda giggled at the memory. "Your lovely books swimming in the puddles. I was mortified that I'd enraged such a beautiful creature."

"Instead, you bewitched me with your lovely pearly hair and ocean-blue eyes." Milenda reached out and touched his sleeve, hoping he could feel the heat of her hand through all the tiers of clothing they both had on. The snow was beautiful, but she was not sure about having to wear these many layers all the time.

The princess had just began wondering how on earth she was going to relieve herself in this frozen desert without freezing, when a cluster of red houses appeared on the horizon. The structures, gathered together as if protecting each other from the icy cold, had snow-white roofs and were bordered by glistening naked trees.

"Örebro." Jaali whispered the word as if he were imparting a secret or a long-forgotten memory. There was a strange, unfamiliar yearning in his voice, and Milenda's heart clenched in sympathy. He was finally home. But was this really his home anymore? The sleigh never stopped, continuing its silent journey down the hill into the tiny village. A dark cloud of anxiety swelled up in the princess's heart. There was no postponing it any longer. She would have to face Jaali's people and deal with whatever their reaction to her might be. Milenda hoped for the best, but the same instincts that had often warned her something was wrong back in Afrika were ablaze, telling her to expect the worst.

***

Jaali

The cold closed its cruel fingers around him, waking Jaali up from the semi-comatose state he was in. The sight of his childhood village proved to be almost too much for him. In truth, he didn't remember much about it or its inhabitants. He wasn't even sure whether the memories of his family were factual or a figment of his imagination. From the recesses of his mind, he saw the face of the woman he believed to be his mother, pearl-colored haired and blue eyed like him. The night he was taken, she had tucked him in tenderly, deposited a soft kiss on his forehead, and bid him a goodnight. He remembered much grumbling from the innocent boy he was then. He didn't want to go to bed. He never did. The world was too full of wonderful things to explore, and sleeping was not one of them. Was he embellishing the memory, or had he been particularly reluctant to go to bed that night? As if he could feel something bad was coming. Something he would never be able to forget or recover from.

"*Wimbo wa moyo*, are you all right?" It was Milenda's hand, shaking him back to the here and now. He had somehow stopped the sleigh and was now sitting in the freezing air, staring down the hill at the tiny red houses clustering together in the center of an equally small village.

Jaali's heart couldn't decide whether to rejoice or dread what was coming. He had finally returned to the place where at the tender age of twelve he'd been taken away from his bed and carried off into slavery. There was no telling if his family would remember him or want him back. After all, he was damaged goods.

Damn! He had finally stopped thinking of himself that way, but now those intrusive and self-defeating thoughts were back. Instinctively, he made a move for Milenda's arm, pulling her close to him, desperate to borrow some of her empowering strength. For a moment, he forgot about himself and focused on his new wife. She had to be scared, or at least worried about their future here in the northern lands.

As soon as his thoughts fluttered to her, the familiar tug of her consciousness called to him inside his head. Their connection was stronger than the simple bond between husband and wife. Theirs was a communion of bodies and souls. Literally. Their minds and bodies were connected in ways nobody could understand. Ever since Yemanjá had awakened Milenda's dormant and ancient gift, the princess had been able to project herself, body and soul, to wherever Jaali was, no matter how far. They still didn't quite understand how it worked, but it didn't matter. That gift had provided him with help and much needed companionship during the Trials.

"Shouldn't we start heading there?" Milenda pointed at the village. From behind the restrictive balaclava, he could see her bright green eyes, glittering with anxiety and concern. He nodded and snapped the reins. The horses resumed their track through the snow.

"Are you nervous?" Milenda asked after a while. She knew he was. Just like he could feel her tugging at his mind, she could feel him. "They will be so happy to see you."

"Will they? Even after they find out what I've done while an *indent*?" His voice was bitter in spite of his resolve to be positive. "After all that was done to me, I'm not the child they knew and loved, whole and pure. I've been broken and sullied."

Milenda pounded her gloved hand on her own leg. "Jaali Asker!" Her voice rose and shook. "I thought we'd agreed never to speak or think that way again. You, my love, are not and were never such thing. You have the purest heart and soul I've ever known. How can you think your family will love you less because of something you were a victim of?"

Jaali dropped his chin to his chest, half in shame for having voiced such thoughts and half in fear that he may be right. "I'm sorry, *msichana*. You often have more faith in me than I do myself. I thought I had put it behind me for good, but being here—facing the possibility of seeing my kin again—made these feelings come crawling back."

With a wiggle, the princess scooted closer to him, looping her arm around his. "They will love you as much or more than they did before you left." Her whisper was barely audible over the sudden gusts of wind fighting their progress down the slope. "I just know it." She rested her head on his shoulder and laughed softly. "You know I'm always right."

Tension effectively dissipated by her joke, they laughed

together as the distant village became more and more real to their eyes, growing in front of them like a balloon being slowly inflated. Jaali's heart contracted again. The dropping temperatures and his anxieties made his breathing labored and unnatural. By the time the sleigh had reached the valley where the village was tucked away, sheltered from the wind by the slopes of several hills, Jaali could hardly breathe.

The bigger structure in the tiny square in the center of town was the community house, the *gemenskap hus*, where the villagers met to socialize and make decisions about their community. The rolls of smoke coming from both chimneys was a good indicator that people were gathered there right then. The memory of late winter afternoons spent in the *gemenskap hus* with his siblings and the other children in town, playing tag around the often cankerous older villagers, came flooding back to him. So vividly and unexpected, he felt as if he was drowning. He gasped for air.

"Are we going in?" Milenda spoke in soft tones, as if afraid to bother the wind that still buffeted everything in its path, even here in the protected valley. "We can't stay out in this cold much longer, and the horses need to eat."

Mjusi had awakened from his deep sleep. He'd been asleep most of their journey there. Jaali wondered whether the reptilian creature had somehow gone into temporary hibernation to protect himself from the icy temperatures. He raised his scaly head, blinked his enormous green eyes, and yawned. Milenda brushed a hand across the top of his head and giggled. "Took a long nap, didn't you, my friend?"

The *mutsi* shook his head and looked around him as

if fascinated by what he was seeing. Everything was so different from what the flying lizard and Milenda had ever known, Jaali had to wonder what was going through their minds as they stared into the squat scarlet houses with tiny shuttered windows and iced-over gardens.

"Might as well do it now." He was talking more to himself than his wife. Making the decision, Jaali jumped off the sleigh, led the horses the short stretch to the *gemenskap hus,* and hitched the animals to the posts. Mjusi flapped his wings and flew a few feet above them, only to alight right next to the sleigh in a storm of dislodged snow and ice. Jaali offered Milenda his hand to help her off the vehicle and onto the snowy ground. He smiled at her, not sure whether he was hoping to soothe her nerves or his.

The door to the community house was a massive wood piece, decorated by large plaques of metal that served the double duty of reinforcing them against whatever attempt at destroying them. In the middle, too high for someone as short as Milenda to reach, there was a metal knocker in the shape of a triskelion formed with three drinking horns. Jaali knew it meant this place was one where creativity and leadership was welcomed, and was to be used only by guests requesting hospitality. It had been placed high up on the door so that children wouldn't use it as a toy, forgetting that not all adults were as tall as most of the Fjordens were.

The sound of metal hitting metal rang through him and echoed throughout the valley. At least, that's how it felt to him. Milenda, still holding on to his arm, shook like a leaf. At the last minute—judging by Herr Karlsson's reaction to

Mjusi—Jaali thought that maybe this wasn't the right time to introduce the rare Afrikan creature to his people and told him to stay outside. The *mutsi* seemed impervious to the cold and walked around the building possibly to relieve himself.

The door creaked open and several curious red faces peeked through the opening. "*Vem är där?*" The voice came from the tallest man, his eyes squinting into the dimming light outside.

They must have looked a fright, with their faces totally covered and layers upon layers of warm clothing making them look almost inhuman. "We're looking for the Asker family." His Fjorden language did not sound natural to him anymore, even though he had taught it in the university for years. "Do you know where we can find them?"

A hush rolled through the space, and for a moment they could hear the crackling of the fire in the hearth inside. The man who had spoken opened the door wide and invited them in. "Come on in, *vänner*." The use of the word *friends* helped Jaali relax a little, his muscles hard as rock with tension. "The Askers are in here somewhere."

Timidly, the couple crossed the threshold into the warmth of the *gemenskap hus*, studying their surroundings and the people who now stared back at them. There were dozens of people in the large hall that held little more than a few trestle tables and benches for furnishings. In the hearth, a monster of a fire blazed and several children huddled together by it.

A young woman, long blonde hair caught under an embroidered scarlet bonnet, took a step forward to meet them.

Jaali hurriedly removed his balaclava and held it against his chest and his rapidly beating heart. She scanned him from head to toe, her thin lips squeezed against each other and her hands hidden under her bright red apron. After what Jaali thought was an eternity, she looked him in the eye and smiled. He blew out the breath he'd been holding.

"*Det är* Jaali. *Vår* Jaali." He understood the words—It's Jaali. Our Jaali—and smiled even though he had no idea who the girl was. She seemed to be just slightly older than he was, but even though familiar, a total stranger.

The rest of the people in the room moved as one body, the rumbling of their steps rushing closer to have a better look at the visitors echoing through the building. He heard his name in the breathy murmurs, a sacred chant of sorts, but didn't know how to react. Had they recognized him? Was his family there with him?

"Jaali, don't you remember me?" The girl, her face lit by a wide smile, pointed at herself. "Maja, your sister." His heart seemed to be trying to escape through his throat. His older sister. His mind tried to find memories of her without much success. "You used to pull on my braids so hard I swear I saw stars every time."

The image came to him blurred and faded, but it did come—a very young Jaali sneaking behind his tall sister and pulling on her long braids as if trying to sound the village bells. He remembered her scream of pain and surprise and the long race through the town square, Maja chasing him under the canopies of local merchants. Tears welled in his eyes.

Maja stepped forward and hugged him, squeezing him against her so hard, he thought he'd suffocate. "You came back, brother." The young woman sobbed, her tears wetting his neck.

Jaali had dreamed about this moment all his life, and yet, it was an empty moment. He didn't feel anything for this sister of his. He barely remembered her. An overwhelming urge to push her away and seek shelter in Milenda's arms came over him.

"I do remember you," he admitted, gently peeling them apart. "Mamma and Pappa?" The crowd of people were all standing around them, their eyes reflecting a mixture of sadness, joy, and expectation. Even the children, who could not possibly remember anything that had happened to him, waited around, quiet and wide eyed.

"*Mamma* passed away two years ago after Elin was taken." Who was Elin? His sister spoke of this girl as if he was supposed to know who she was. "Too much heartache for a lifetime. And *Pappa* is out fishing with some of the other men. He'll be gone until the snow begins to melt, I'm afraid. He'd be here if he knew you were coming."

Unable to take it anymore, Jaali reached out for Milenda's hand. His princess was still fully covered in the wintry clothes, her dark skin hidden and her eyes shining in confusion. She had just recently begun learning his language, and Maja was speaking too fast. He pulled her to his side and slid his arm over her shoulders.

"This is my wife, Milenda." His voice echoed a little too loudly. Nerves were getting the best of him. "She doesn't speak much Fjorden yet, so please speak slowly when addressing her."

Maja approached her and shook her free hand enthusiastically. "Glad to meet you, sister. Why don't you make yourself comfortable?" Then, she turned to the children behind her and yelled out, "Go fetch them some hot coffee and something to eat. Quick."

Two of the older women brought a couple of chairs for them to sit down, and Maja signaled Milenda to remove her coverings. Jaali felt her tremble. This was the moment they both had been dreading. There was no avoiding it. It was almost oppressively hot in the room, and by now the princess must be roasting underneath all the clothes. Jaali removed his coat and handed it to Maja who then turned to Milenda.

She glanced up at him, her eyes pleading, her hand shaking. "It's all right, *msichana*," he whispered, beginning to unbutton her coat. "It has to be done." His use of her language drew some curious looks from those who were close enough to hear.

Her coat came off first, then her gloves, and last the balaclava—the one layer standing between her skin and the world. The gasp that spread through the crowd in a wave, rising and falling, was not unexpected but still unsettling.

Milenda stood trembling, her beautiful brown face shiny with nervous sweat. She looked so young and so helpless, Jaali felt the urge to pull her into his arms and protect her from the probing glares of his own kin.

"She's one of them!" The words were thrown at them

with the hardness of rocks. "Your wife is a *odjur*, a *duivel!*"

Jaali's head snapped up at the sound of that word. His owner had been a true *duivel*, a devil who used and abused him without a qualm. No one would address his sweet and brave wife the same way. He hugged her tighter still.

"Do not call her that. Milenda's my wife, and you will respect her as such." He didn't know he had it in him to stand up to a crowd like that. A crowd of strangers. It hit him hard, the realization his own people were nothing but strangers to him.

"But, Jaali, she's one of them. Look at the color of her skin." Maja's face had turned a sickly hue of red, and her lips set into a frown. "How could you have married an *odjur*? Did she buy you in the market like a piece of meat or furniture?"

With his wife tucked in against him, Jaali lifted his chin and straightened his back. "I fought for her and won her love. She's not a Mabaya warrior or a slaver. Mark my words. She'll be the one ending this cruel trafficking. So treat her well, treat her with respect. She deserves nothing less."

A man shoved his way through the ranks of the crowd to face them. He was tall and burly, his muscles barely disguised under the thick wool of his shirt. "I'm Arvid, the *Genomdrivare* of this town." The enforcer's voice was deep and low. "In the name of the law, I must take the slaver into custody."

"Did he just say he's going to arrest me?" It was the first time Milenda spoke, her voice shaken. "Do they think I'm a

Mabaya warrior? Didn't you tell them I'm not?"

Her green eyes were pleading, reflecting a desperation he had never seen there before. His heart exploded.

"You'll do no such thing!" He didn't raise his voice, but the tone left little doubt to his sincerity. "You'll find us a place to spend the night, and as soon as I can get us situated, we'll be out of your town. I'm a Fjorden, and I remember clearly that, according to our laws, I can be the one to have custody of my wife if it so pleases me."

The crowd seemed as surprised about this sudden knowledge of local laws as he was. How did he remember that? He had been a small child when he left. All the years of isolation in Natale, immersing himself in scholarly books, seemed to have finally paid off. The *Genomdrivare* nodded, and with his arms still protectively around Milenda, Jaali followed the man toward the front door.

"I can offer you the barn behind the *gemenskap hus*," he said. "For a few days, but I suggest you move on. The people are not happy you brought an *odjur* into our midst."

Following the big man into the cold outside, Jaali and Milenda shook—out of fear, exhaustion, disappointment. The big barn house stood dark and inhospitable like the town people. Not that he had expected a fantastic welcome, but he certainly had hoped for at least friendly faces and a warm bed to sleep at night. It looked like they would be sharing their first night back home with the beasts instead.

Arvid opened the large wooden door and signaled them inside, feeling his way along the inside wall. "There's a lamp here somewhere," he mumbled. Soon, the light of a small oil lamp introduced them to their sleeping quarters—a rather vast and cold space, populated by horses and cows who, startled out of their sleep, whined and mooed in a cacophony of wordless complaints.

"There is a loft up there." Arvid waved his arm toward a ladder resting against one of the sides of the barn. "You'll be warm enough there, and the animals won't bother you." In spite of the earlier reaction, the man seemed almost apologetic as he spoke then. "You may not remember it anymore, Herr Asker, but Fjordens are superstitious people. It comes with being helpless victims for far too long. I harbor no hate for your wife, black skin or not. But I'm the law in this town, and if the others demand it, I won't be able to stop them from arresting her."

They both understood the power of superstition and fear. Afrika and the Outerlands may be oceans apart, but they had that in common. Jaali thanked the man and led the princess to the ladder.

"I'll bring you something to eat in a while." Arvid turned around and left them.

"We should call Mjusi inside too." Milenda had finally found her voice, however small it sounded. In the confusion, he had forgotten about the *msitu* still outside in the cold. "I don't think he feels the cold like us but still—"

Jaali cracked the heavy door open and called the flying lizard until his familiar green head and eyes appeared from the dark. "Come inside and warm up."

When the *Genomdrivare* came back with warm bread, butter, and two mugs of hot coffee, Milenda had already curled underneath the old blankets they found in the loft above, Mjusi lying beside her whimpering softly. Jaali came down from the loft, took the food from the man, grateful that there was at least one person in town willing to lend them a hand, and after bidding him goodnight, crawled in beside his wife.

"I'm sorry, *wimbo wa moyo*." Milenda's voice rose in the darkness of the barn and soothed his soul like a caress.

"What are you sorry for, *msichana*? You have done nothing wrong."

"I'm sorry that because of me your return home wasn't as happy as you hoped. As I hoped it would be." Her head, nestled in the crook of his neck, smelled of spice and honey. "What are we going to do now?"

Jaali brushed his lips against her forehead. "We wait for my father to return and then—we'll see. We must find a place of our own. In the morning, I'll ask Arvid if there is anywhere we can stay. We have coin, we can pay him."

"We'll be all right, we'll be fine." Milenda chanted the words like a prayer. Maybe she was praying to Yemanjá, mother and protector of all creatures. Or maybe she was trying to convince herself of what was beginning to sound more like a dream that would never come true.

EXILE

The glow from the lamp Arvid had brought them the night before had long faded, and the space was dark except for slivers of faint light coming through the cracks in the wooden walls of the barn. Milenda didn't want to move. Cocooned within her husband's warm arms and under the blankets, the chill in the air didn't bother her. Her hands, which had been left uncovered for a while, were cold, and she tucked them in beneath her. Ever since they'd approached the Arctic Circle, the nights had become longer and longer, as if trying to deny the sun its right to shine.

"We have to get up sometime, *msichana*." Jaali's breath tickled her neck, and her *matangazos* immediately responded with fire, a sudden burst of heat along her markings that made her shiver in delight. "I know it's tempting to stay under these warm blankets, but we have to find a place to stay before the winter is over."

The princess groaned, knowing all too well he was right.

Their welcome by Jaali's childhood town left a lot to be desired, and it was to their own benefit to leave as soon as possible. Memories of the night before in the *gemenskap hus* made her cringe. The language was still mostly foreign to her, but the facial expressions and body language was universal—the people of Örebro were not pleased with her presence there.

"They hate me." She had recognized words like *duivel* and slaver thrown at her, along with looks so pointed and sharp they had cut into her heart as effectively as knives. She understood their hatred, sympathized even, but it still hurt.

"They don't know you." Jaali pulled her closer to him, his heat transferring to her body, so unaccustomed to this kind of temperatures. "If they did, they'd love you as much as I do." Not much chance of that happening if they had to hide somewhere away from town. "They're strangers." Her husband's voice changed from the comforting singsong tone he always used when trying to make her feel better to a somber, sad tone.

Milenda scooted and turned around so she could face him. As she moved, the icy air crept beneath the blankets and clothes, covering her with goose bumps. "What do you mean, they're strangers? They're your family, your people."

Jaali smiled, a sad smile that bespoke of his beautiful soul. "I don't know them at all. We may be related by blood, but I don't have any memory of Maja or my father. I barely remember my mother."

"Give them a chance. Give yourself a chance, *wimbo*

wa moyo. Time heals all wounds." She cupped his cheek and brushed her lips on his, backing away slightly to look into his eyes. There was a storm brewing in those ponds. She yearned to erase the pain she saw churning to the surface again.

"Maybe it's time for me to start praying to Freya again." He chuckled softly, kissing her nose. "Pity Yemanjá does not rule in these parts."

Should she risk worrying him more by telling him of the demigoddess visit? Or should she just keep it to herself, considering that so far there were no signs of divine intervention of any kind. She told him in the end. Every detail of her strange conversation with the Mother, including the plan to foil any attempt at a new heir to the throne.

"Mama Nyeusi is in on it?" Jaali's voice rose an octave or two. "I can't even imagine your old *iyalorixá* doing something so devious."

Milenda laughed. She could. Mama Nyeusi was all about fairness and justice. As long as whatever she was putting in that tea didn't hurt the new queen, she would not hesitate to follow Yemanjá's orders.

Light came a bit brighter through the cracks and the small window on the roof. The soft whining of the horses and the mooing of the cows confirmed morning was on full blast and it was time to get up. As if guessing the change in the mood, Mjusi uncurled from his cat-like position, yawned loudly, and almost hit them with his tail as he began moving around, ready to go outdoors.

"He probably needs to go relieve himself." Jaali's eyes

followed the track of the *msitu* across the loft.

"He already did. I heard him getting up a few hours ago."

Jaali snapped his head around. "Where did he go?"

"Somewhere in here. I would be very careful where I step." Milenda knew Mjusi would have found a corner away from them to do his business, but it was too tempting to play around with her husband, wise about so many things, but also naive about others.

There was not much to get ready for. They had both slept in their day clothes, too cold to change. After letting Mjusi out, they folded the blankets, slipped into their heavy coats, and waited for Arvid to show up. He had promised to take them to a settlement where they could possibly find a more permanent place to stay. When they heard the telltale clanking of the heavy lock being opened, they moved closer to the ladder, ready to climb down as both light and arctic cold flooded the barn.

"Jaali? *Bror*?" Milenda recognized Maja's voice, soft and hesitant. She would never forget the voice of the girl whose eyes had bulged out of her pretty face when Milenda had removed her face covering. What was she doing here?

Jaali looked at his wife, a question dancing in his eyes and mouth half-open in surprise. "Maja?"

The barn fell into almost darkness again, and Milenda heard the muffled steps of the young woman crossing the space in their direction. The wood of the ladder creaked, and soon the woolen-covered head of Jaali's sister appeared on the loft, her pink cheeks almost glowing in the dim light.

"What are you doing here, Maja?" He had forgotten to

speak in his own language, and it took him a few moments to realize it and repeat the question.

Maja climbed onto the loft, and after a short, nervous glance in Milenda's direction, began a quick, agitated conversation the princess couldn't follow. She recognized a few words—sorry, surprise, and wife. Jaali seemed shell-shocked, listening to the torrent of words coming from his sister, his hand still holding on to Milenda's.

When Maja's voice finally quieted, both brother and sister stared at the princess as if they expected her to respond in some way.

"What's going on?" She had no idea what they had said or wanted her to say. Frustration made Milenda's *matangazos* glow below her clothes, and she tucked the *nguba* tighter around her shoulders. "For all that's sacred, what were you talking about?"

Belatedly, Jaali gave her a comforting hand squeeze and smiled. "Sorry, *msichana*. Maja was telling me she was sorry for what she said in the *gemenskap hus* last night." The young woman nodded as if she could understand her brother's words. "She was surprised and shocked, and allowed her suspicion for people of your color to get the best of her. She wants to help us find a place where we can be safe."

Maja spoke again, a rat-a-tat-tat of words Milenda couldn't follow. Tired of feeling lost in this conversation that so obviously centered around her, she reached out to Jaali. She hadn't done it since the Trials, so it came as a surprise that she could still do it. As she did, tendrils of her own mind stretching out to his, and she felt what he felt, understood what she could not otherwise. Her husband stole a shocked look at her, but then relaxed into the knowledge of what she was doing.

"Arvid found a house on the other side of the valley where you can stay in some safety," Maja was saying. "It's close enough that you can come into town any time you need, but away from suspicious eyes." And prejudiced minds, Milenda thought.

"What do you think, msichana?" His voice echoed in her head as clearly as if he had actually uttered the words. Which he hadn't.

For a second, the princess allowed herself a moment of joy at the intimacy of being connected with the man she loved that way. Fears that they might have lost that magical soul and mind link, now that the Trials were behind them, had been plaguing her. Even though the Trials had been tough for both of them, curiously she still missed those days when they were so far away from each other and yet so close together.

"Do you believe her? Is she really sorry she called me those horrible things last night?" Milenda wanted to believe Maja had a change of heart overnight, but circumstances had taught her not to be too trusting. She was well aware that what people said and what they actually thought were two very different things. The Elders had exalted her like the queen she was slotted to be, and yet behind her back they had been planning her demise and replacement.

"Don't remember much about my sister. She looks sincere." Jaali moved his eyes to focus on her for a moment,

and her heart sang as it always did under his blue scrutiny. *"Besides, what do we have to lose? We need a place to stay away from here. You saw the looks they gave you last night."*

Maja's gaze bounced between the two of them. Could she tell they were having a silent conversation? Or was she confused by the lack of response from either of them?

"We'll do it." Had she really said that? In Jaali's native language? She didn't know she knew those words.

Jaali seemed as surprised as she was, his mouth falling slightly open and his brows arching high above his eyes. Maja fixed her stare on the princess, a subtle cringe crossing her face, as if not pleased with what she was seeing. No, she didn't trust that girl, Milenda decided. There was something not right about her behavior. But they did need a place to stay where they could have as close to a normal life as they could, instead of sharing a sleeping space with animals.

"She speaks our language?" Maja cocked her head to the side, her eyes narrowed and her lips pursed. "I thought she could only say and understand a few things."

Jaali seemed to be at a loss for words, rubbing at his eyebrow with a finger and eyes never leaving his wife's. Milenda smiled in spite of everything. Apparently, their mental connection had transferred his knowledge of Fjörden to her. She was now able to understand and respond. She suspected Yemanjá's hand in all of this, but they would wonder about the small miracle later.

"I do speak the language." She had found the confidence buried deep within herself. She was strong, and she wouldn't let these people and this situation drag her down. "When do we leave?"

With the help of Arvid and a rather shifty Maja, they were on the road to their new home in a small settlement called *Hoppas*, a name Milenda chose to take as a good omen. Settling in a place named Hope seemed to be the first good sign since they had arrived in *Isvärld*. She hung from Jaali's arm, suddenly giddy with happiness and optimism. Maybe things wouldn't be so bad after all.

Maja stayed behind with the excuse she had to take care of her children. Jaali had started at the information, and Milenda felt it—the overwhelming anguish at feeling like an outsider among his own people, his own family. There were nephews or maybe nieces, and yet his sister didn't seem too keen at sharing that information, as if she preferred to keep her family away from her own brother and his abomination of a wife. His heart contracted with pain, crushing hers. How she wished there was something she could do to wipe the ache from his chest, to erase the pain from his eyes.

What Maja and Arvid had claimed to be "not too far" ended up being over an hour's journey, and the settlement nothing more than a handful of houses spread thinly across the snowy valley. Milenda's heart dropped a few inches. This was no town, not even a hamlet. They would be isolated from the rest of the world as if contaminated by some dangerous plague. In fact, that's exactly what it was, except *she* was the plague.

Jaali, feeling her turmoil, pulled her closer on the sleigh. "Look, the house is like a little enchanted cottage in a fairy tale." Milenda smiled at his attempt at cheering her up. The red house they were quickly approaching was nothing more than a wooden box, the sharp vee of the roof covered in snow and ice, and a small window by the large brown door. It was a miniature model of the barn they had slept in. "But it's ours. Alone."

In his mind, she read excitement and anticipation at finally being alone together. They had been around people from the moment they had married, and the idea of semi-isolation was an attractive one. Milenda giggled as she thought of being with her husband the way they had been during the Trials, when no one suspected she was with him. Free to act however they felt like. Free to love each other, fully and completely.

"It's beautiful." The little house sat by the frozen creek that ran the extent of the valley, from the thick woods behind to the hills beyond. Even from a distance she could see animals that resembled gazelles frolicking in the snow-covered grasses. "What are those?" She pointed in the direction of the woods, squinting her eyes against the weak sun.

"Red deer. There are a lot of them in these woods." His handsome face opened in a wide smile. "I remember chasing them when I was little." His voice trailed off, sucked into his memories, a dreamy glaze coming over his eyes.

The sleigh stopped in front of the house. Milenda noticed another small window on the side, framed in white painted wood as the one in front. "Here's your dwelling." Arvid jumped off the vehicle in a fluid move that belied his size and offered her his hand. "I must return quickly.

Darkness will be here soon, and I would like to be safe and sound back home when it does."

Jaali carried their chest of belongings to the front of the house and thanked the big man. "We're grateful that you were willing to help us."

"Can't protect you forever though, Jaali Asker." The man shook his hand and then Milenda's. "You stay away from the others as long as you can. There is hate and resentment in their hearts, the result of too many shed tears. It won't be easy to dissuade them from the idea that your wife is evil."

The couple nodded and thanked him again.

"Inside there is everything you need for the next few days. You'll have to go fishing or hunting after that. There is plenty of rabbit and deer in the valley and woods. Maybe a boar if you're lucky, but I would stay away from them if I were you." With those words, he climbed back on the sleigh and left them standing by the small square house in the middle of a vast, lonely valley with not a soul in sight.

As soon as the sleigh was but a small dot on the horizon, Mjusi who had flown behind them, wisely keeping his distance from Arvid, landed beside them with a big splash of cold snow. The winged creature seemed to be at home in the icy landscape of *Isvärld*.

"He likes the *theluji*. Look how much fun he's having with it." The *msitu* was rolling around in the cold whiteness, flipping big chunks of snow up in the air and catching it with its tongue.

Jaali laughed, tucking Milenda under his arm and planting a light kiss on her cheek. "Are you ready, *msichana*?"

Milenda turned to face him, her gloved hands reaching out for his pale face. "With you, *wimbo wa moyo*, I'm always ready for anything."

* * *

JAALI

The growling was so intense, Jaali thought Mjusi was in some kind of pain, but when he went to check on him, the flying lizard was by the door frantically asking to be let out.

"Something is going on with the *msitu, msichana*." At first, he had resisted the idea that Mjusi was indeed acting strangely, but he couldn't deny it anymore. The creature was fidgety and anxious most of the time, groaning or growling low in its throat as if mourning or yearning for something.

Jaali opened the door for the creature, and with a big flap of his majestic wings, the *msitu* flew away. With a sigh, Jaali closed the door and joined his wife by the hearth, a corner brick structure crowned by a large white canopy that led the smoke out without allowing the cold air in. The house was bright and cheery inside despite the rather plainness of the outside. It reminded him a bit of his *hema* in Natale, tiny but comfortable and artsy in some ways. By the fireplace, which was also the stove, there was a small kitchen counter— really just a narrow table with storage below, some shelves above, and a sink with running water.

On the opposite wall, there was a bed nestled on the wood-paneled wall, a closet, and an underbed storage cabinet. Most of the interior was painted white, with some yellow here and there, giving the whole space a sunny feeling that belied the gloominess of the northern winter days. On one of the side walls, the only outward protruding area, there was a small bathroom heralding a toilet and a sink.

"I will build us a proper shower." Jaali knew how much Milenda enjoyed the amazing showers of her royal residence. He was determined he would build her the best shower a princess could have under the circumstances. He was good with carpentry and knew about plumbing. All he needed now was access to good wood. A project for another day.

"What are you daydreaming about?" Milenda's voice, still slurred with sleep, pulled him out of his reverie. "And did you mention Mjusi?"

Jaali smiled, watching his jewel stretching like a cat in their bed. *Their* bed. There was a simple wonderfulness to those words. Until now they had shared beds that were not theirs, and been around others who could easily interrupt their intimate moments. Here, they were by themselves, alone in their own place. Milenda had brought plenty of coin with her, courtesy of her father, and they had insisted on paying for the humble house in the middle of the frozen valley. It was not perfect, but it was theirs.

"Mjusi was going crazy trying to go out." He followed his wife's movements as she climbed out of bed, naked as the day she was born, and wrapped her beautiful body with their wedding *nguba*. His blood raced faster in his veins, yearning to draw her into his arms and make love to her again. "There's something going on with him."

Milenda sat on one of the chairs by the small table and nibbled at a piece of bread, her leg folded under her, looking blissfully unaware of the effect her bare skin was having on her husband. "I told you something was wrong." The blanket slipped off her shoulder a little more, exposing her glowing *matangazos*. Not so unaware after all, it seemed. She winked at him, and he laughed. His princess was not so innocent anymore.

In a single stride, he was by her, kneeling beside her chair, his hands sliding gently up the side of her thighs. "My sweet Jewel, you have the gift to drive me crazy with a single look." She giggled and covered his hands with hers, bending down slightly to capture his lips.

"What are we going to do with all this free time?" Milenda's breath tickled his lips, and he kissed her again.

The *nguba* slipped off her back completely, revealing her perfect petite body. Jaali moaned. *"Msichana*, I can think of a million things we could do right now that would be very pleasurable for both of us." As if to demonstrate it, he lowered his lips to her breast and lingered there for a moment. Her whimper of pleasure almost undid him. "But—" Milenda groaned in protest. "—we'll be out of food in the next day or so. I must go hunting."

Grasping the edges of the wedding blanket, Jaali covered his bride, giving her one last kiss before getting onto his feet. His body and soul were aching for hers, but he knew his words to be true. They must not allow themselves to be blinded by their love for each other and forget they must work hard to survive in the hostile environment they lived in. It had been a couple days since Arvid had dropped them off, and the food was running scarce. Jaali had found a bow and arrows in the closet, but no gun. It would have to do. He hadn't used one of those in years, but he was hoping he still knew how. Their survival might very well depend on it.

Milenda put on clothes while he tried not to let his eyes wander to the body he loved so much. He still found it hard to believe that the tiny woman he now called wife had been the one to slay all his demons—demons he had carried around within him for more years than he could remember, and from which he never thought he'd be free. No more fears about himself, no more doubts. Milenda's love had effectively cleared him of all the self-defeating thoughts and beliefs gathered like a monstrous cloud throughout his years as an *indent*, a slave.

"What exactly are we going to hunt for?" The princess was now fully dressed in a strange combination of colors and cultural styles—a heavy, fur-lined tunic over the typically vibrant *kanga* dress.

"What do you mean *we*?" His head snapped up, the bow he was testing almost dropping from his hands. "You're not going with me."

Her intense green eyes pierced him. "I'm going with you." It was not a request. The royal tone of her voice left no doubt as to how serious she was. "I need to learn how to do this. What if something happens to you and I'm left alone for a while? Do you want me to starve? I'm not a helpless little girl, and you know that."

Jaali suppressed the smile creeping onto his lips for fear she'd misunderstand it. She was right of course. His Milenda had never been the helpless kind, and she should learn how to survive in the semi-tundra where they lived. But the fire in her eye and her rigid, defiant stance were such a sweet reminder of what they had gone through together, it was hard not to smile.

"But we only have one weapon." The weak protest escaped his lips before he could stop it. Part of him—the part that still wanted to shelter and protect his beloved—couldn't help it.

The princess, her hair flying and bouncing with every movement, produced a big knife from the counter and held it in front of her face. "Not to worry. I'm pretty handy with this."

She sounded so convincing, he did laugh this time, bending at the waist. Perplexed at first, Milenda joined him soon after, her crystal-like chuckles cascading out of her in waves of sound. Jaali loved her laughter. He loved her everything.

"Well, Mrs. Asker, you need some heavier clothing on you and boots. This is no walk in the palace gardens." He deepened his voice and tucked his chin in. "And you must follow orders, soldier. Do you understand?"

Milenda saluted him like the old soldiers in her kingdom, and then stuck her tongue out at him. One minute a grown-up, the young woman that she still was another. The fact that she had to grow up too fast made him sad because it reminded him of his own life—being thrown to the wolves as a child with no way to defend himself. Milenda had been thrust into adulthood by the fact she was a future queen with a price on her head. She may not have been abused like he was, but she had grown up alone and unloved just like him.

After covering themselves with what seemed the appropriate amount of clothes, they left. The snowshoes attached to their boots made for slow walking, but without them, they would sink deeper into the layers of snow. Jaali was hoping to be able to keep Milenda out of danger, at least until she was more used to the cold ice and the lack of body freedom she was so used to in Afrika. Going from wearing a thin *kanga* to layers upon layers of tight and thick material that restricted movement could not be easy for her. He had been born in these parts and was having trouble getting used to it himself.

They didn't have to go too far into the woods to find fresh rabbit tracks on the snow. Jaali gestured to her to stay to the side in case the rabbit took off running as he advanced quietly, bow at the ready. A few steps further and a couple of snow-white creatures hopped and ran with all their might from under a tree. Jaali drew the string back and lifted the bow in front of him, aimed, and shot. The arrow flew gracefully until it hit its target. His shoulders relaxed, and he lowered the bow, relieved he still remembered how to use the weapon.

Milenda fumbled her way to the collapsed bunny. "We got one." He smiled at how young she sounded. "Look, *wimbo wa moyo*, we got one." She held up the dead rabbit like a trophy, her white teeth standing out in contrast with the dark balaclava she wore.

As if on cue, something dropped between them, lifting a great wave of snow into the air and startling them. Once the snow settled, Jaali approached the large dark pile just as Mjusi landed by them with a loud flap of wings. The *msitu* had been busy hunting as the small mountain of furry animals laying on the snow seemed to point at.

"Mjusi, you went hunting for us." Milenda's surprise and pride colored her words as she rushed to wrap her arms around the large lizard's neck. "I love you."

Jaali examined the pile of dead animals. It was quite an impressive yield, with rabbits mixed with squirrels and even a pine marten. They would have meat for a while. "Thank you, Mjusi. This was very nice of you. Did you eat yourself?"

The winged creature nodded and nuzzled Milenda with its scaly snout. A stab of irrational jealously came out of nowhere and left Jaali feeling guilty. The *msitu* had been Milenda's only friend for most of her life and had helped them on more than one occasion. Sometimes Jaali wished he knew Milenda as well as the forest lizard did, but he knew there was no reason to be jealous. The love Milenda felt for the creature was more than deserved.

"Thanks to you, friend, we'll have a feast tonight." Jaali tied the animal paws together and pulled them up and over his shoulder to carry them to the house. "Of course, we must still skin them all."

Milenda straightened. "What? Skin them?"

Satisfied that he had managed to spook her a little, Jaali

chuckled under his breath. "Unless you want to eat them with the fur still on."

The princess abandoned Mjusi and began tracking behind Jaali, who was already heading back. "You're going to do it, right?"

Mjusi flew over their heads toward their small home. Jaali's smile stretched wider. "No, you'll do it. You told me you were good with the knife."

"What? No, no. I can't skin those furry creatures. They're too cute. I can't do it." Her words spilled out in a torrent of nerves and repulsion. "I'd rather starve."

Not letting her see his grin, Jaali continued his track across the valley. "Well, I guess we'll have to starve then, because I have no skills with the knife at all. I was counting on you."

Milenda sped up and went around Jaali to look at his face. Even though he couldn't see her face through the knit of the balaclava, he could see her forest eyes opening wide as she realized he was teasing her. "You wicked man. Scaring me like that."

She hit him with a gloved hand, and he laughed. "Sorry, *msichana*, but I couldn't resist. You should have heard yourself—"

As she tried to punch him again in protest, Jaali grabbed her hand and pulled her to him. "Wicked, wicked man." The accusation was uttered like a caress, and his heart began the usual gallop.

"I'll skin the beasts." He gulped, the air becoming harder to breathe as her eyes latched on his. "I love you, *msichana*,

I'd never make you do something you hate."

Milenda's teeth made another appearance. "Son of a crooked shaman!" she exclaimed. "How do your people ever make babies with all these clothes?"

Jaali almost dropped his load. "Is that an invitation?"

She turned on her heels and began running—or what running looked like in those snowshoes—toward the house. "Meet you at the house."

The temperature was no match for the heat those words caused in his body. He was on fire, but the weight of the dead animals didn't allow him to go any faster. So, he plodded away, anxious to reach home and wrap his arms around the crown jewel of his heart.

WITCHCRAFT

MILENDA

"I'll be fine." The words sounded sincere, but her heart didn't believe them even as she uttered them. The idea of Jaali traveling all the way into town by himself and leaving her alone made her nervous on so many levels. She hadn't been separated from him since the Trials, and the idea of even a minute without him made her heart ache. It was ridiculous to think that they would never be apart again, she knew. But it just seemed too soon.

"It won't take too long, *msichana*." She was not sure whether he was assuring her or himself. Jaali didn't seem too keen on the idea either. "I'll be back before sundown." Sunset would be in less than four hours, and Arvid would not bring him back if there was even a slight chance of being caught by night. Milenda was bracing herself for her first night alone.

Determined to show him how comfortable she was with the idea of being left alone, Milenda locked her hand around her husband's arm and pushed him gently toward the waiting sleigh. "You go in peace, reacquaint yourself with your sister, and then come back to me safe and sound. I have Mjusi. We'll be just fine."

Jaali allowed her to lead him to the sleigh, and after a quick peck on the lips, he climbed onto it and settled beside Arvid who seemed more than anxious to get on the road. *"Stay in and stay warm."* His thoughts touched her own with the softness of a caress, and she smiled. Thanks to her gift, they would never be truly separated.

Milenda watched the sleigh vanish into the horizon, anxiety building up in her chest like an ugly balloon full of noxious gases. She chided herself for being silly, but she couldn't shake the feeling something terrible was about to happen. Shaking her head, she went back in the cabin, closely followed by Mjusi who had been acting like a mother hen ever since the arrival of Arvid and his vehicle.

"Stop acting like you're my guardian or something, Mjusi." Milenda patted the creature's head and grinned. "I'm old enough that I don't need a mother." Not that she had ever had one. Her memories of her mother were nothing but dreams since she had died—no, she was killed—when Milenda was but a baby. Mama Nyeusi was the closest thing she had for a mother, and even she had come late into her life. No, she did not need to be mothered. She had made it this far, and she would keep doing it.

She scanned their small living space and sighed. It would probably be a good time to organize things a bit. Not that the place was messy. Jaali was almost fussy about cleanliness and tidiness. Having grown up in the palace with a legion of servants to do her biding—and pick up after her—the princess was just learning that in spite of her rather magical gift, nothing got cleaned and tidy by the grace of magic. Some of her nightclothes were still lying on the floor by the table where she had thrown them during the night while she lost herself in her husband's lovemaking. In the sink, a couple dirty dishes lay witness to their frugal breakfast. The door to the bathroom was opened, and vestiges of Jaali's attempts at building them a shower lay on the floor, bits and pieces of lumber salvaged from the woods, rope and rocks. Milenda smiled, sighed again, and began her track around the house to do what she had very rarely done in Afrika—clean her own mess.

It took a lot less time than she expected, and soon she was sitting by the small window with idle hands and a wandering mind. Without even realizing she was doing it, she reached out to Jaali. He was still on the sleigh, but she could see Örebro in the distance. Instinctively, Milenda held on to his arm, sitting next to him and giving him a start.

"Msichana, what are you doing here?" His voice echoed inside her head, and she smiled. This never got old. Jaali was trying not to look at her, she assumed for fear of looking crazy. Arvid sat on his other side, eyes peeled on the snow-covered road ahead, hands on the reins. *"What if he sees you?"* They had never attempted to reach each other in front of other people, she realized. There was no telling whether others could see her or not.

Milenda was about to leave when Arvid suddenly turned

around and his eyes locked with hers. His eyes blinked fast and furious, and his face, already white as ivory, turned a sickly shade of gray. Milenda thought better of vanishing in front of his eyes and offered him a tentative smile. But the bulky man didn't seem to notice. His grasp on the reins was so tight, the horses stopped in their tracks with a lot of huffing and stomping.

"How is she here?" Arvid's voice was shrill, and his eyes bulged out of his sockets. "We left her behind. How is she here now?"

Jaali's skin had turned transparent. He looked frantically from one side to another, as if searching for a logical explanation why his wife, whom they had left behind over an hour ago, was now sitting next to him in the sleigh. "Don't panic, Herr Arvid. There is a perfectly good explanation." Milenda raised her eyebrow. This she wanted to hear. "She didn't want to stay behind and climbed in under the blankets."

The princess snickered. That was ridiculous. She was small, but even she couldn't hide there. Besides, she was wearing her house clothes. No coat, no boots, no hat. She was obviously not dressed for the outdoors. "We might as well tell him the truth."

Jaali didn't seem convinced. His eyes still bounced from Milenda to the lawman, mouth slightly agape and a sheen of sweat on his forehead. "I don't know, *msichana*, maybe it's not a good idea."

"What do you mean the truth? What is going on here?" The man still had the wild look in his eyes that Milenda imagined someone would have if faced with a ghost. "What kind of a sick joke is this?"

The Jaali reached out to touch the man's arm in an attempt to calm him down. "No joke, Herr Arvid. We mean no disrespect." But the man was getting more agitated by the minute, brushing his hand frantically on the back of his neck and licking his lips until they were red and swollen.

Milenda took the lead. "I was given a gift from Yemanjá a while back. She gave me the power to project myself to wherever Jaali is."

"Who's this Yemanjá? A witch?" Jaali's body went rigid, and she knew this was not a word the Fjorden took lightly.

"No, a demigoddess like Freya." As she spoke, Milenda could tell the story sounded more and more outrageous. After all, if someone had told her the same story a year ago, she would have laughed and thought they were mad. "She's an Afrikan deity who took a liking to me and Jaali and has been helping us."

"Freya does not interact with humans. She cannot be bothered with the small affairs of mortals." In other words, he was calling them liars. "This is witchcraft." Once again, Jaali blanched at the word, and she knew with certainty they were treading in dangerous territory.

The man made to grab her, but Milenda snapped the link between her and her husband. She was back in the cabin, alone and trembling, unsure of what had just happened and what it meant to their future there. She didn't dare go back to Jaali, but she was also aching to offer him the support he undoubtedly needed right then. He had looked so stricken, almost scared, when the other man had used the word "witchcraft."

In Afrika, the word didn't have much meaning. Hers was a world where magic was accepted and believed in naturally. All Afrikans knew there was magic in the world. There was magic in each human being. And the deities of Afrikan tradition all used magic one way or another to keep an eye on their mortal children. However, Arvid's reaction and Jaali's own fear of the word told her things were different here. Natalians were superstitious, but it looked like Fjordens were even more so.

For the rest of the day, she tried to read and clean. She even walked outside in the freezing cold, hoping to achieve some peace of mind, but her heart wouldn't let her. Inside of her, this irrational fear of something evil brewing grew to such size and girth, she could barely breathe. What if those horrible people in town had hurt Jaali? Or held him in town so he couldn't come back to her? There were so many what-ifs.

"Well, Yemanjá, where are you now that I need you?" She spoke to the air, pacing around her house barefoot and delighting in the feel of fur under her feet, like a comforting hand soothing her nerves. "And what about this other goddess, Freya? Is she going to help us or allow Jaali to fall into danger from his own people?"

Tears burned in her eyes, blurring her vision. She didn't want to cry. Milenda hated feeling hopeless. In the past, she would have reached out for her husband, but now she couldn't. Something in the way he had looked at her told her it would be the worst thing she could do.

Mjusi scratched at the door, asking to be let in, probably feeling her emotional turmoil. As soon as he was inside, he paced around her legs, whimpering softly and nuzzling her with his scaly snout.

"I'm okay, my friend. Just worried about Jaali." She inhaled deeply and then exhaled slowly. "Everything will be fine." A quick glimpse through the window told her it was beginning to get dark, which meant only one thing—Jaali was not coming back that night.

Forgetting to eat, Milenda crawled in bed and hid her face on the pillow. Mjusi flapped his wings and landed gently beside her on the bed. With the usual soft whimpering, the creature curled upon himself, his back against Milenda's and fell asleep. It was going to be a very long night.

***

JAALI

The man looked like he had swallowed a prickly pear. His alabaster complexion turned a mottled shade of purple, and his cheeks puffed up to match his bulging blue eyes. Jaali knew they were in trouble. Milenda should have never reached out to him when he was with company. Granted, she didn't know Arvid would be able to see her just as clearly as he did, but it had been a major mistake.

"You married a *duivel* and a *häxa.*" Jaali had often lovingly called Milenda a little witch, but there was no endearment in the way the other man was uttering the word. Memories, long thought forgotten, of witch hunts in his village popped into his head and made him want to run. "You brought evil into your village and family, Jaali Asker. Why would you do something like that?"

The horses were jittery, sensing a change in mood, and the sleigh jerked this way and the other, making his body slam into the big man's. "It's not witchcraft, Herr Arvid. It was a gift from a goddess just like Freya. Milenda doesn't have magic at all." How else could he explain what his countryman had witnessed?

"It's *trolldom*, witchcraft." Arvid was not listening. He scanned the horizon with crazed eyes that bulged out of their sockets. "You've brought a *häxa* into our midst."

Jaali contemplated jumping out of the sleigh and taking his chances with the cold, but he knew it would be foolish. Not only would he never make it back to his wife in time, but it would make it look as if Arvid's claims were legitimate. Somehow he would have to convince the others Milenda was but a goddess's favorite, not a witch. Images of women and men dragged to the main square of the village in shackles, displayed in shame and then stoned to death for the use of the dark arts invaded his memory and made him cringe in fear.

He had forgotten how superstitious his people were. Years of absence and abuse at the hands of others had softened his familiarity with his own countrymen. It had blurred the ugly side of his cultural heritage and made it fade into the background.

Arvid drove the sleigh to the town square, jumped out into the fresh snow, and ran to ring the town's bell. In no time at all, dozens of curious and worried faces appeared at the doors of the houses nearby, quickly followed by the soft, muted padding of those who lived further from the square. A rumbling of low voices reminded Jaali of the day Milenda had announced her intentions to marry him to the populace of Natale. It had been an unsettling sound, pregnant with uncertainty and anxiety.

This was worse. The humming of voices reached his ears with such a sense of dread, he would have sworn he could see the darkness of their words. People stared at him as if he was an animal in a zoo, an unfriendly creature who could pounce and attack them at any time.

"People of Örebro, something of grave importance just came to my notice." Arvid had raised his arms above his head, speaking in the formal way that Jaali recognized as the traditional way to share serious news. Around him, the people of Örebro had closed ranks, and Jaali was caged in should he decide to flee. "I was just made witness to an act of witchcraft, black magic."

The crowd let out a loud collective gasp. Jaali's mind frantically searched for the right words that could protect his wife from mass hysteria, but couldn't find any.

"Jaali Asker brought a witch into our midst." Another gasp. "I was willing to concede that the *duivel* he calls his wife was not like the others who have preyed on our children, but after what I just witnessed, I can no longer support that idea. I saw her—with my own two eyes—

appear out of nowhere and from miles away into our sleigh, only to disappear again."

The murmuring of voices rose in a wave, and Jaali was suddenly pinned in place by the angry eyes of his countrymen. "What do you have to say for yourself, Jaali Asker?" It was his sister, Maja, carrying a baby on one hip and holding on to a toddler with the other hand. His blood relatives. A growing sadness took residence in his heart, weighing him down. Even his own sister seemed to be ready to think the worst of them.

"My wife is not a witch." The voices grew louder, and Jaali had to raise his voice to be heard. "The Afrikan goddess, Yemanjá, gave her the gift to do that. It's not magic, and it's not dark and evil. She means no harm at all. All we want is to be allowed to live our life in peace."

"What about our peace?" Maja's face was beet red as she spat the words that may forever ruin any chances he and his wife might have at happiness. "Those black *duivels* come and hunt down our children, take them into slavery never to return. And now we must welcome one of them? One who is a witch?"

The voices were growing frantic, panicky. "I was one of those children. Have you forgotten?" Jaali yelled with all his strength. He must convince this angry mob that Milenda was not here to harm anyone. "Milenda was the one who saved me, who loved me, and brought me back from a dark place and into the light. My wife is not a witch; she's not a *duivel* of any kind. She's a *malaika*, an angel." His people didn't seem convinced, their eyes hard and cold like the icicles hanging from the roofs. "Please, we're here in peace. We came here to meet my family, not to harm anyone."

There was a moment of silence, and Jaali allowed himself a moment of hope.

"I say my brother has been bewitched." Hope crushed into dust, Jaali raised his trembling hands up in front of him to no avail. "We go get the witch and keep my brother from her until her power over him fades."

The taste of bile rose to Jaali's mouth, and chills ran through his body. He scanned the square, searching for a break in the crowd where he could possibly escape through, but there was no way out. Even as he stood there, shaking in anger and fear, the crowd was closing in on him, their expressions matching the falling darkness.

Someone grasped his arms and pulled them behind his back. "I'm taking you in, young Asker, for your own safety," Avrid said as he pushed him through the ranks of the angry mob. Then he turned to the crowd and announced, "We will go first thing tomorrow morning and pick up the witch."

Jaali resisted, thrashing this way and that, more in protest than actually trying to escape. "Please, don't hurt Milenda. She hasn't done anything wrong."

"You'll thank us later, Jaali Asker. Once she doesn't have a hold on you anymore."

The big man half dragged him to a nearby building where he was thrown into a small, dark room with only a cot in the corner, a table and chair, and a tiny bathroom. Jail. They were putting him in jail. The fight had gone out of him, mostly because it was useless. He was only one against a crowd of people very willing to believe he was under a spell. He crawled into a corner of the room, sat with his back against the cold wall, and hung his head while Arvid locked the door behind him, leaving Jaali in total darkness.

What was he going to do now? Come morning, they would be heading to his little house with weapons in their hands and hate and fear in their hearts. A fatal combination. If they didn't kill Milenda on sight, they would drag her like an animal into town and expose her to all kinds of indignities before killing her in front of every eye in town. That's how witches were dealt with in his world. No, not his world. Not anymore. He could no more accept the prejudice of the Fjordens than he could the cruelty of some Natalians.

He had to warn Milenda. By now, as the impeding Northern early night fell upon the land, she would be certain he wasn't coming back until the next day. He could almost see her in her nightclothes, her black hair loose and wild, framing her beautiful face, going to bed wondering about his welfare. She always worried about him. He often thought it was ironic that in their fairy tale she was the knight in shining armor and he was the damsel in distress. Maybe it was time he donned some armor as well.

Trying to remember how it worked, Jaali thought of Milenda. More than a thought, it was a yearning, a call, a desire so vivid and so strong she wouldn't be able to ignore it. It took a few seconds, but he felt it—the swoosh of air moving against his face, the prickling in his fingertips, the speeding of his heartbeat.

"*Wimbo wa moyo*, you're here." Milenda, still fully

dressed, sat up on the bed they had shared, Mjusi lifting his head next to her. "When did you get in?"

Jaali had a moment of hesitation. Maybe he had dreamed the whole thing. Maybe he had been asleep next to her and had a nightmare. But then he noticed his clothing, and his heart lurched in his chest. This was no dream.

"*Msichana*, you have to leave." He sprinted to the bed and held her in his arms, rejoicing in her body heat, her coarse hair tickling his face and neck. "They're coming for you."

She looked up at him, eyes still blurry from sleep. "Who's coming for me? And where can I leave to?"

"They think you're a witch, and they're coming in the morning to get you." Jaali stumbled over his words, not sure where to start. "They've thrown me in jail."

Milenda straightened in his arms, her back going rigid. "How dare they? Is that how they welcome their own people?"

"They won't harm me. They think you have put a spell on me." A bitter chuckle left his lips. "Once the spell is broken, they will let me go. You're the one who's in danger. They will kill you."

Strange that they had come this far to escape the Elders and their plans to kill both of them, just to fall prey to the same fate. The irony didn't escape him.

"But where can I go? No matter what village I go to, they will shun me. I can't hide the color of my skin any more than you could in Natale." She was right. There was no easy solution for her situation.

The great winged lizard had slid out of bed and curled itself around both their feet, growling softly but insistently as if trying to tell them something. Jaali stared at the creature, a new hope rising in his chest.

"Mjusi will protect you. You pack warm clothes, some food, and go hide in the woods." Jaali's head was swimming with ideas, all jumbled up together as he tried to make some sense out of them.

"Are you crazy? It's the middle of the winter. I'll freeze." Milenda slumped against him, defeated in spite of the fighting words.

"If you stay here, you're as good as dead." He hated himself for having to tell her that, but there was no time for platitudes or white lies. "Out there you have a chance. You won't be alone. Mjusi will be by your side. He's been out there by himself many times. I think he may have a hiding place somewhere."

Her hands went limp against him, her beautiful green eyes avoiding his. "What about you?"

Jaali wanted to tell her everything would be all right. He wanted to hold her in his arms and love her until morning broke through the dark of night. But he knew he couldn't. If she didn't leave soon, all their hopes of a life together would be little more than a fantasy.

"I'll be fine, really. I'll help you pack."

Milenda couldn't take much with her. Once they got to the thick of the woods, the little sleigh Jaali had built with twigs and branches wouldn't be able to navigate through the brush anymore, and the princess and her *msitu* would have to carry it. Warm clothes and food were the most important items. They still had some canned items left in their small pantry and plenty of meat.

"No meat," Jaali had declared when Milenda tried to pack some of it in the sleigh. "It will attract predators. Mjusi will hunt for you."

Jaali retrieved the bow and arrows from the closet and draped it over her overly dressed shoulder. She was ready. At least, as ready as she would ever be. They walked outdoors, their breath visible in the dark air, and stood facing each other.

"Promise me you'll be safe." Milenda, always thinking of his well-being, melded her lips against his in a furious, desperate kiss. "I love you, *wimbo wa moyo*."

Jaali licked his lips, tasting the sweetness of her on his tongue and missing it already. "I love you, *msichana*." He turned to the *msitu* and smiled. "You better take good care of our jewel, Mjusi." The animal growled and nodded its head. Jaali turned to the princess again. "Here we go again." It came in a whisper, moist with the threat of tears. "I'll come and get you soon."

Another fierce kiss and she was gone. The dark, cold jail cell surrounded him again, oppressive and lonely. His princess would be all right. They had gone through worse; they could do it again and come out victorious on the other side. Jaali wanted to believe that, but his stomach had tightened into a small, hard ball, and his lungs struggled to breathe. His eyes closed, his breathing slowed, but peaceful sleep did not come to him that night. Instead, memories of the

Trials replayed in his dreams. He tossed and turned through the night, restless and scared for his heart's song who was alone, fighting for survival in the snowy wilderness.

FREYA

Milenda had never been scared of the dark, but the darkness took on a whole other dimension when trudging through feet-deep snow, dragging her own weight in supplies. The small, weak torch she had found buried deep into the closet was no match for the thickness of the black outside. Even Mjusi seemed daunted by the challenge ahead, growling softly behind her. Once in a while he would do that funny puffing he'd been doing since they arrived in the northern lands. Little clouds of mist came out of his mouth, a strange ghostly shape against the cover of the night.

"We're almost by the woods, my friend." She was not sure she was trying to soothe the *msitu*'s nerves or her own. The forest loomed just ahead, large and even darker than the night, the giant evergreens standing jealous guard over whatever secrets the woods hid. Milenda had a moment of regret—having been stupid enough to reach out to Jaali when she did—but shook it off quickly. No time to cry over what should or could have been. Time to focus on what it was and what would be.

As soon as they arrived at the edge of the woods, Milenda picked up the contents of the small sleigh she had been dragging through the snow and hid it carefully behind some bushes before carrying on deeper into the forest. "We must go far enough and then find a place to rest safely." Mjusi perked up his ears and took the lead. Even though he normally flew, Milenda was certain he knew his way around the trees. There was no telling what dangers these woods held. Jaali had told her of bears, but those were probably hibernating this time of year. She had also heard of a wild cat called a lynx that could be deadly. *Think only of the positive, only the positive.* She repeated the mantra a few times, breathing rhythmically and slowly, and her muscles unclenched, a wave of relief going through her.

After an hour or so of treading through the thick woods, the princess was lost. If she had to go back where she came from, there would be no way she could do that. *Good, that means my tracks will also be hard to follow.* Another wave of doubt hit her. The locals were probably great trackers, and she was a foreigner from a totally different world. What did she know about snow? About this glacier-carved land, as beautiful as it was terrifying.

"You got Mjusi." The voice came from all around her. Her muscles relaxed at the sound of Jaali's voice in her head. His breath caressed the side of her face. *"Mjusi will take care of you until I can come to you."* She turned toward the voice, but there was nothing there but a soft glow

perforating the blackness of the night. She smiled. Jaali may be far and unable to help her, but he was always with her.

"Let's keep going, Mjusi." Her energy recharged, Milenda wanted to take no risks. She had come this far to be safe with the one she loved, she was not going to allow another people's superstitions to take that away from them. "Take me where you think it will be safe. I trust you, my friend."

It was hard to tell how long they walked, feet and hands numb by the cold, since the northern night lingered for most of the morning, as well. After a few hours, the terrain became rockier and steeper. Mjusi was taking them into the mountains. Was that where he had been flying to every day since they got there? What was it about those mountains that attracted the winged beast so much?

At one point, the flying lizard stopped and became agitated, growling and shaking his head. Milenda took a few steps forward and examined the bushes in front of them, moving the branches to the side and peeking behind them with her torch. It was a cave. Large by the looks of it and well hidden from other animals or humans. "Well done, Mjusi. We can both hide in here and sleep."

Milenda half crawled into the rocky enclave, closely followed by her friend. Yes, this would do nicely. The space was wide, even if not very high, and almost warm in comparison to the temperature outside. Not a speck of snow in sight. "Perfect." Well, as perfect as she could reasonably expect to find. They went as far inside as they could and laid down curled around each other, keeping warm. The *msitu* fell asleep right away, but Milenda, in spite of her exhaustion, couldn't. She had too much in her mind—ideas, fears, and longings. Tears rolled down her icy cheeks, and she was surprised they didn't turn into ice instantly.

"Crying is not going to help you." The female voice made her jump. Mjusi, startled out of his sleep, moaned a bit, but fell asleep again. Whoever was there with them in that cave did not seem to alarm the great lizard.

Milenda looked around, but could see nothing but darkness. "Who are you? Show yourself."

A small clicking sound preceded a flash of light. The cave was inundated in a soft glow. At its center, there was an unfamiliar woman—tall, muscular, and beautiful. Her hair fell in thick, long silver cascades over her ivory shoulders. Something was off about this night visitor, but Milenda couldn't quite say what.

"Close your mouth, girl. It's very unbecoming." Her words rang familiar to her. Who had said almost those exact words to her before? "Aren't you going to ask me how I got here?"

The woman's voluptuous body was covered in very little, and large patches of milky skin lay bare and exposed to the cold. Was this who she thought it was? "Freya?" Only a goddess would be able to stand in subzero temperatures half naked.

"Well, I'm impressed with your deducing skills." Were all demigoddesses sarcastic? "My sister, Yemanjá, made me promise to watch over you. I don't normally take too much of an interest with human affairs, but she was very persuasive."

Milenda smiled at the memory of just how persuasive the Mother was. "I'm honored that you've taken me under your protection." Mjusi was snoring happily next to her, his great green chest rising and falling to the sound of his sighs and snorts. "Can Mjusi not see or hear you? He hasn't reacted to your presence."

Freya laughed, throwing her head backward. "He can see me all right. He knows he has nothing to fear from me. I wouldn't hurt one of the great wyverns." The word meant nothing to Milenda, and she was tempted to ask further questions, but decided against it for fear of annoying the fickle goddess.

"What can I do then—" She stopped, not knowing what exactly to call Freya. Yemanjá was the Mother, Creator of all that was living. What was this goddess? Jaali had told her she was the goddess of love, sex—this had made her snort in laughter—fertility, and wealth. But what should she call her?

"Lady, call me lady." That clarified one question at least. Milenda rubbed her cold hands together and smiled sheepishly, more than a little uneasy about the presence of the demigoddess there. "I was told you were smart, but you've done the dumbest thing you could have done, and you've put yourself and one of my children in danger."

The princess's hopeful mood deflated at the words. "I know, my lady. I didn't think others could see me. In the past, we've always been alone."

"Well, it was pretty stupid." Freya didn't seem to mince words or care whether she was hurting anybody's feelings.

Jaali's assessment of the goddess as fickle seemed more than appropriate. "That said, you are under my protection, and for reasons I can't fathom, one of my children is head over heels in love with you. I understand you're a future queen to your people." It was not a question. "You must start thinking like one and stop acting like a child."

Was this what it felt like being chided by your mother? Milenda didn't know since she had very few memories of her own, but she decided that if that was the case, she hadn't missed anything good. Her cheeks and *matangazos* burned full force.

Freya tilted her head to the side, her eyes scanning the princess's covered shoulder and neck. "Those are strange markings you have, girl." Could she see through those thick layers?

"The Nyota, my ancestors, were known to have these *matangazos*—markings that respond to emotions." What did Freya care about her ancestors or the fact that her spots lit up like a chandelier whenever she was scared, happy, or sexually aroused?

"I heard of such things many lives ago." She was suddenly pensive, her perfect goddess face clouding over. After moments passed, Freya lifted her eyes up to Milenda again and smiled. Not the kind, warm smile of the Mother, but coquettish—the smile of someone who knows many others admire and envy her beauty. "In the morning, after you and your wyvern rest, you'll head up the mountain. Mjusi will know the way. He'll take you into a place where you'll be safe for now."

"What about Jaali? They have him in jail." It came out as a squeal of desperation.

"They won't hurt your boy, I promise." Her voice was finally serious, and at that moment, Milenda believed her. "I'll come to see you again soon." The goddess seemed ready to leave, but at the last second, she turned to Milenda again. "And remember, you're a woman now, a queen. Act like one."

Milenda blinked, and Freya was gone. Mjusi stirred in his sleep but never woke. What had she called him? A wyvern? What was that? And how come she knew his kind? Her eyes began closing, heavy as lead, and her head dropped to Mjusi's back. She would think on it tomorrow. Or was it already today?

* * *

JAALI

The rumbling of voices and footsteps woke him up. There was a thread of light sneaking in through a crack in the shuttered window, and he finally could see again. Jaali stretched, his muscles aching from the night curled up on the hard mattress of the cot, and focused on the noise. The villagers were gathering in front of the prison by the sounds of it.

He threw the blanket to the side, jumped out of bed, wincing as his bare feet hit the hard floor, and ran to the window. There was no way he could open it. It was shuttered from the outside in thick, good, solid wood. But there was a small crack, and he was able to peer into the town square where a large group of men and some women were gathered. The mob of blond Fjordens seemed agitated, thickly dressed in furs and carrying assorted weapons—he spied two guns, a couple of bows, and a variety of heavy staffs. Jaali mumbled a prayer to Freya. He hoped Milenda had listened to him and gone as far from their house as she could.

A metal clank announced a visitor, and he ran to sit on the edge of the cot, trying to look casual. He didn't want to give his people the satisfaction of seeing him in a torment of worry. Arvid came through the door, so tall he had to duck. He had a bowl of something steamy in his hands.

"Here's something for you to eat," he said, putting the food down on the small table by the wall. "I won't be back for quite some time, but my wife will bring you some more food later today." He hunched down and pulled a blanket and a towel out of his bag. "Here's an extra blanket, and you can wash up if you wish."

From behind him, two women appeared—one carrying a basin and the other a large pitcher. They were both tall and pretty, one older than the other—mother and daughter perhaps. They walked around the big man and deposited their load on the table side by side with the food. Jaali noticed steam coming out of the pitcher. He was right. They had no intentions of hurting him. He was one of their own, one of the kidnapped children, and they would protect him with all their might. Milenda was a different matter though—a foreigner who in their minds was also a witch. She was in grave danger.

Jaali forced himself to be polite. "Thank you for your kindness. May I ask to have the shutters open, please? I'd like to have some light."

Arvid didn't hesitate. Waving a hand at the youngest woman, he sent her out, and within a few moments, the light of the winter sun had invaded the whole enclosure with all its majesty. Jaali took a deep breath and felt better, stronger.

"My wife will make sure you're comfortable while I'm gone." The man pointed at the older woman. "Make no mistake. She may look small, but Lara is as strong as an elk, and she's armed." Jaali stifled a smile. Lara was very tall, especially compared to tiny Milenda who barely reached his shoulders. He had no intentions of trying to subdue the woman. Or anybody. What good would that do?

As the threesome left him to his own devices, Jaali heard another rumbling sound. It was his stomach. He hadn't eaten since much earlier the day before. A delicious cinnamon smell wafted from whatever it was they had brought him to eat. His mouth watered. He sat on the only chair in the small room and attacked the porridge-type mush in the bowl with the ferocity of an angry bear. Reluctantly, he admitted to himself that the food was delicious—creamy, thick, and sweet. With each spoonful, he felt more energized and calm.

His mind wondered to his wife, and his stomach clenched again. Was she safe? Had she made it through the freezing cold of the night? Milenda was strong and determined. He had no doubt she could do it, but the weather of his native country was not something she was used to and, therefore, a natural enemy she had few weapons or defenses against. Jaali, porridge gone and stomach full of warmth, stood up and checked the window. No one around. He wanted to reach out to his wife, but was nervous about someone walking in on him while he was gone. He still had no idea what he left behind when he was with her. What if he couldn't do it at all? After all Milenda would have to be thinking of him as he reached out. There was always the chance she wasn't, but considering their situation, the odds were on his side.

Hesitantly he reached out to her, first forming a mental image of her beloved face and then remembering how her amber skin felt against his. He lost himself in the memory, and tingles of pleasure covered every surface of his body. He chuckled softly. His wife was indeed a witch. She didn't even have to touch him for him to go into fits of ecstasy.

"So, sex is all you remember me by." The voice, thick with annoyance, made him snap his eyes open. Milenda was standing there, her fur-covered arms crossed in front of her, a frown pulling the corner of her lips downward. "I'm running for my life, and my husband is imagining me naked in bed with him. Nice."

Jaali covered his mouth to hide a smile. Gods, he loved that tiny, fiery woman! "Of course not, *msichana*. I love you for so much more than that." He opened his arms and drew her overstuffed body to him. "No chance of sex with all these clothes anyway." The comment earned him a punch in the arm. His lips sought hers, and for the next few seconds, the world around them ceased to exist. This was theirs and theirs alone. No one would ever change that.

Mollified by the kiss, Milenda smiled as their lips parted. "Are you okay? Have they hurt you?" She scanned his body, as if looking for signs of any kind of abuse.

"I'm fine. I told you, they won't hurt me." He brushed a hand over her cold face. "I'm in a warm room with plenty of food. You're the one in danger." For the first time since his arrival, Jaali searched their surroundings, looking for dangers. They were outdoors in a small clearing in the mountains judging by the incline, but there was no wind and the cold was bearable. Mjusi was nowhere to be seen. "Where's the *msitu*?"

She waved a hand up in the air—he must be hunting or scanning the terrain. Milenda was sitting on a large tree trunk, and she had the carcass of a small animal by her feet. The bones were picked clean. She rolled her eyes at his look of surprise. "Mjusi went hunting earlier. This is his gift for me. Remember that time in Natale when he gifted me with a disgusting dead rodent?" They burst into laughter at the memory. "At least this time he picked something I could actually eat." Her voice softened with her eyes. "Thank you for teaching me how to clean game. I would starve now if I didn't know how."

Jaali's heart melted at the expression in her forest eyes. "I'm sure you'd figure it out if I hadn't." He sat next to her, holding her hands. "How are you doing?"

Milenda told him how Mjusi had found a good place for them to hide overnight, how Freya had honored her with a visit.

"Freya came to see you?"

"Last night. She's a bit different from Yemanjá." Milenda bit the corner of her lip. "I'm still wondering if it's a good thing to have her on our side. She didn't seem very… altruistic."

Jaali was amused by how careful his wife was about her word choice in case the goddess was listening in. Not much chance of that. Freya was not known for her interest in human affairs unless she profited from it somehow—or if there was a good-looking young man available for the plucking. Her appetites were well known among his people. Yemanjá must have a lot more power than he had given her credit for if she was able to convince the Lady to protect them. Or maybe Milenda's survival was of an even bigger importance than he had imagined.

"I can't stay long. Arvid's wife is keeping an eye on me, and I'm not sure what she'd see if she was to look in while I'm here with you." He nestled his lips on her neck, above her *matangazos,* and kissed her, earning a gentle moan of pleasure from Milenda.

"She would find you sleeping." Milenda's lips stretched into a bright smile. "That's what my maid told me when she came in my room one time I was with you. Don't go yet, *wimbo wa moyo.* Wait until Mjusi comes back."

They talked quietly for a while, hand in hand, the weak sunlight shining down on them as if blessing their love. After all they had gone through, these were the moments they cherished, moments stolen from an otherwise turbulent and dangerous life. When would they be free to enjoy more of these moments without fear hanging over them like an ominous storm just waiting to explode?

Mjusi came back, his great wings creating gusts of wind as he landed by them. At the sight of Jaali, Mjusi came to nuzzle his hand in greeting. Jaali patted his head between his big green eyes. "Thank you for watching over our princess, Mjusi. I'll be eternally grateful to you."

"Jaali, what does the word wyvern mean?" Milenda asked him out of the blue.

"Wyverns are a species of creatures that haven't been seen in centuries." A memory nudged him. What had the inn keeper called Mjusi? "Dragons. Wyverns are commonly known as dragons." Jaali's eyes wandered to the *msitu*. Could it be? He seemed awfully small for a dragon. "Why do you ask?"

"That's what Freya called Mjusi last night. A wyvern." Milenda laughed. "Do you think he's a dragon?"

Jaali stared at the flying lizard, not sure of what to believe. It was a lifetime ago, but he did remember seeing illustrations of dragons in schoolbooks before his kidnapping. Later, in the university, he had read books about the great wyverns, and yes, there was definitely a resemblance. He couldn't believe he had never noticed it before. Mjusi was not very big, smaller even than a zebra, except for his wingspan, which was awe-inspiring. But he did look like the illustrations in the old books. Could it be? Was Mjusi one of the great Northern wyverns?

MAJA

The higher they climbed, the harder it was to breathe evenly. The terrain had become rockier even as the tree cover became sparser. Mjusi, in a show of solidarity, stumbled ahead of her instead of flying. Milenda couldn't help but swell with love for this creature who had always been there for her, even when her own father had not. The *msitu* seemed to know exactly where he was going, allowing Milenda to relax in the knowledge she was in good hands.

By now the people of Örebro had surrounded and invaded their private space, the first place Jaali and her could call their own. *It didn't last long.* Milenda sighed, far from resigned, but with no other option but to accept it and move on. It was not easy—accepting something she viewed as unfair. Her whole being revolted the same way it had revolted against the hold the Elders had on the population of Natale—a power made that much more unsettling because it came from feeding superstitions and myths with no base on reality. She would have her day with the Elders, she was sure of it. But for now, she must face another type of injustice.

Milenda's legs complained under her weight as she lagged half the load of supplies they had packed. Mjusi had gracefully volunteered to carry the other half, a welcome relief for her sore back and arms. She looked upward and her heart quivered a little—was she imagining it or were they getting closer to the top? There was no telling what awaited her there, but at this point she didn't care anymore. She was just happy to be able to stop the steep climbing they had been doing for the last who knows how many hours.

Mjusi became more animated, which only confirmed her suspicions that something up there meant a lot for her beloved *msitu*. He tried to hop over the last few yards and started a small avalanche of loose rocky soil. "Careful, friend. You're going to bury me before I can get to the top." Milenda laughed as she dodged the debris careening down toward her. "What's up there that makes you so excited, anyway?"

The *msitu* turned his head to her and uttered a funny sound, something between a growl and a whimpering. Her friend was happy, she realized. She had never seen him so excited, and for a moment, she forgot the reason why they were struggling to focus on his joy instead. She sped up, cursing the loose rocks under her feet that made her track up the steep face of the mountain so much harder. Mjusi was already at the top, flapping his wings and squawking like a bird.

"I'm coming, I'm coming." She huffed and puffed, out of breath and cringing at the electric-like shocks her muscles created with each simple movement.

With a painful but determined swing of her arm, she threw her makeshift bag over the ledge and pulled herself up into what Mjusi seemed to think was the Promised Land. She shook the dirt off her clothes, shook her aching legs and arms, and then glanced up to where the *msitu* had already scampered off.

She almost fell off the edge. "Son of a wicked shaman!" Fighting to get a firmer balance over her wobbly legs, Milenda blinked and stared at the sight in front of her, her hands covering her wide-open mouth.

Mjusi, hooting and yapping like she had never seen him do before, had joined a group of creatures that left no doubt as to their kinship to the flying forest lizard. The other *msitus* were as different as they were alike, and they all stared at her as shocked and surprised as she was. There were more Mjusis in the world after all. What had Freya called them? Wyverns—a family of magnificent wyverns stood a few yards away from her.

"Mjusi, you found your family." Milenda felt tears burn in the back of her eyes. Her flying friend had always been as lonely as her, maybe even more so. She had no friends and only a distant father, but she at least was surrounded by fellow humans. Mjusi had no one beside her. Joy bubbled from her heart up her throat and into tears that rolled freely down her cheeks. "So happy for you, my friend."

One of the wyverns growled loudly, throwing his

massive green head backward, and for a moment—and only a moment—Milenda wondered whether they were dangerous. Mjusi happy yapping told her otherwise. He would never bring her into the middle of any danger. She was safe.

Milenda watched the family of wyverns in wonder. Two of them were about Mjusi's size, but the other two were much larger, more than twice his size. One of them was female. Milenda had no idea how she knew that, but there was something about the coloring of its scales, a deep green speckled in purple, the way it moved the massive wings protectively over the smaller ones. A mother maybe? The other was definitely a male, his gaze on hers, almost defiantly, as he paced around the others, reminding her of the strut of the peacocks back home. His forest green head was topped with needle-sharp spikes of ocher and vermilion that followed the curve of its neck all the way down his back, stopping shy of the tail. The other two played around with each other, chasing the other's tails, biting playfully at each other's snouts. *Is Mjusi still a young one of the species?*

As if he had read her thoughts, the *msitu* came to her and nuzzled her legs. Milenda laughed. "There are more of you after all."

Her winged friend pulled on her hand and coaxed her closer to the others. It made her a bit nervous. She had known Mjusi her whole life—she trusted him. These other creatures were unknown to her and, even though she wanted to trust them implicitly, she couldn't.

"Are you sure they won't hurt me?" Mjusi was still

poking her with his muzzle, trying to get her to move. He made a little sound and shook his head. "I hope you're right. I don't feel much like being your friends' dinner."

She allowed herself to be pushed all the way until she could feel the great creatures' body heat. The cold around them seemed to have faded away some, and she was tempted to remove a layer of clothing. The one she thought was the male stretched his head forward and sniffed her.

"I'll call you Tausi," she whispered, hoping the wyvern wouldn't take offense at being called peacock. He barely seemed to register her voice, focusing on smelling her clothes and snorting little puffs of smoke once in a while. Strong heat emanated from him as if he carried a fire inside. "You're like a mini-volcano with wings, aren't you?" His head snapped up suddenly, and she almost lost her balance. Milenda braced herself, but the wyvern shook his head and walked away. "I guess I must have passed muster."

The female came next. There was a gentleness mixed with fierceness in the way she walked and waved her long tail. Her green eyes were not as hard as the male's, gazing at her with interest but also a certain amount of tenderness. Milenda's thoughts went to Mama Nyeusi and how her own brown eyes could be hard and soft at the same time. Something inherently feminine somehow. "I'll call you Mama Msitu," Milenda whispered into the wyvern's ear, her hand cautiously brushing along the top of her scaly head. She too was warm to the touch, almost hot. "Are those your young ones?"

The two small wyverns, just slightly smaller than Mjusi,

were chasing each other around like two puppies. Milenda laughed as the lighter colored one tried to grab the other's tail with his mouth and earned a slap on the face instead. Did this mean that Mjusi was still a juvenile in *msitu* terms? She had always assumed that her friend was older than she was since his size had not changed much over the years. Now she was beginning to realize that his kind didn't grow at the same rate as humans.

Mjusi sat by her legs, protective as always, but his big green gaze was intent on the two young ones and their playful games. "Go play with them, Mjusi." He turned his neck to look at her and tilted his head. She smiled. "Go. It's okay. Tausi and Mama Msitu will keep me company."

In fact, both wyverns had lost interest in her and walked away, their long, fierce-looking tails wagging slowly and widely behind them. Milenda sighed and stepped back to give them a wide berth. For better or worse, this was going to be her hideaway until Jaali could somehow convince the villagers she was harmless. Several caves of differing sizes hugged the perimeter of the mountain ledge where this family of flying creatures made their home.

Her eyes followed the slope of the land over and behind the caves as it reached higher into the sky. The mountain seemed endless, as if it would stretch forever into the heavens above. Maybe into Freya's lair. Not that she knew where goddesses lived. It was not in anybody's best interest to engage the deities into too long of a conversation or ask too many questions, Mama Nyeusi had always told her. Their ilk bored quickly and angered even easier.

Tired and sore—and starved—Milenda made her way into one of the smaller caves, peering inside for signs of life. It was empty. None of the dragons seemed to have claimed it, so she ducked under the low ceiling and dropped gently onto her knees by the opposite wall. It was warm on that ledge, as if the beasts produced their own heat and created a kind of shield against the winter cold. She removed her heavy, bulky coat and dropped it behind her before stretching all the way onto the soft, dirt floor. The coat cushioned her head like a pillow, and it didn't take her long to start drifting off to sleep, her heavy eyelids closing slowly against the light. From outside, the muffled noise of shuffling and the occasional yelp from the small wyverns soothed her nerves. For the first time in the last few days, she was at peace.

As she drifted off to sleep, the warmth from a familiar body spooned her from behind, and she molded herself to its curve. "Jaali," she whispered already half asleep.

The soft waft of warm air on her neck reminded her of another time. It seemed like a lifetime ago when, still unaware of her special gift, she had reached out to Jaali in her sleep. Then she had thought she was dreaming. She moaned softly, her *matangazos* warming up along her neck and shoulder.

"Sleep well, *msichana.* " The caress of Jaali's voice lulled her further into sleep. "I love you. Forever and always."

The words formed in her mind, but she couldn't be sure she actually uttered them as slumber embraced her with all its might. "I love you too, *wimbo wa moyo.*"

***

Jaali

The stomping grew in a crescendo, pulling Jaali out of his trance-like state. His mind had been with his wife on top of the mountain and his body half here, half there. He had stopped trying to make sense of it a while ago, his brain incapable of completely grasping the concept of what Milenda's gift could do. It was easier to accept and let it go.

He shook his head, still in a daze, and trained his attention on the sound of many footsteps and voices outside his prison. Jaali jumped out of bed and ran to the window. The villagers were back, and they didn't sound happy. The deep snow was not enough to disguise the displeasure and anger in their steps, their booming voices reaching his ears clearly even through the thick glass.

The men and women returning from their hunt were joined by the ones who had stayed behind. Voices rose and fell until their eyes all turned to where he was jailed. "He must have warned her." Jaali didn't like the sound of that. Would they now also accuse him of witchcraft?

The mob turned on their heels and headed to the building that served as the local prison. Belatedly, Jaali ran back to the cot, hoping they hadn't seen him at the window. His heart was ready to jump out of his chest. The certainty he had felt before—that they wouldn't hurt him—was wavering as the loud voices approached and the door opened, spilling the angry mob inside. Jaali placed his hand on his knee to stop it from shaking and made himself stare into Arvid's eyes.

"How did you do it?" The big man spat the words, his hands on his wide waist.

Jaali willed his voice not to shake. "Do what? What are you talking about?" Then, breathing in a dose of courage, he lifted his chin defiantly. "Where's my wife? What did you do with her?"

Arvid stepped forward and bent down so his face was at the same level as Jaali's. "She wasn't there." Each of the words came out isolated, as if he was having trouble controlling them. "What did you do?"

Afraid his legs wouldn't hold him, Jaali stood up nevertheless. "What do you mean, what did I do?" His voice was soft but assertive. "I was stuck in this jail all this time. Ask your wife. She came and fed me." He pointed at Lara, standing just behind her husband. "Tell him, go on, tell him."

Arvid looked back at the blonde woman. Every eye in the room followed him.

Lara shrugged and shook her head. "He was here all the time. He ate and he slept." She scanned the room and threw her hands up in the air. "It's the truth. He didn't go anywhere or do anything. I checked on him several times."

A frustrated and still angry Arvid stared back at Jaali, eyes on fire. "You must have done something. She wasn't there."

Jaali couldn't help himself. "Good. She's not stupid. She noticed your reaction when you saw her in the sleigh.

She knew better than staying put and waiting for ignorant people to come and take her."

He knew it wasn't wise to throw jabs at those who held him captive, but he was angry. Furious at the fact that once again, they were victims of superstition and fear of anything different. That yet again they were on the run, hiding from those they sought to befriend. Running in fear of his own people.

"Unfortunately, she's used to thinking twice before trusting anyone. She's been betrayed, hunted, and undermined. Did you really think she would be sitting at home waiting for you?" All the anger and frustration he had felt since the posse had left the village poured out of him in a tidal wave of words. "I thought we'd be safe here with my own people. That my family and neighbors would be happy and welcome the one who saved me. And yet, here we are, treating Milenda just as badly as the slavers treated me and the others who were kidnapped with me. As if she's nothing. Worse than that, as if she's... garbage."

"Your wife is a witch."

The way the big man spoke those words told Jaali there was no guilting them into seeing reason. There was fear and hate in each syllable, as if the simple act of uttering those words may bring doom upon the village. Jaali knew what fear could do. Fear fueled inaction when action was needed and projected a mask of reason onto what made no sense at all. Fear made Natalians accept the cruelty of the Trials and the tyranny of the Elders without question. Fear was pure poison.

Jaali exhaled deeply and sat on the edge of the cot again, his hands holding on to the edges as if afraid he may do something he would later regret. There was no point in trying to reason with them right then. Their minds were muddied by their fears and superstitions. He could only hope that Freya would indeed protect his wife as Yemanjá had promised, but it was hard to trust a goddess who allowed her children to be taken as slaves to faraway lands. A goddess more interested in her sexual trysts than the well-being of her own people.

"Fine. Believe what you will." His grasp on the edge of the cot was so tight his knuckles were white. "Begone. If you're going to keep me in prison, then leave me be."

The crowd hesitated, exchanging furtive looks, before turning their backs on him and streaming out of the door. Arvid lingered behind, his stance not as tense as of a few minutes ago.

"I know what I saw, Jaali."

Jaali looked up at the man, his shoulders hunched forward slightly. "No, you don't. You really don't, Arvid. That's the tragedy of it all. You have no idea what you actually saw."

"Explain it to me then." The others had all left, the icy wind sneaking through the open door.

"You saw two people who love each other so much their souls are connected, entwined like two vines around each other. Never really separated, never really alone. Two bodies, one soul." He missed the other half of him, the part that completed him and made him brave and daring, willing to face and survive the merciless *Jangwa Pori* desert.

Jaali missed his princess, his jewel. "But that you'll never understand. You see only evil where there's nothing but light. Leave me alone."

Arvid opened his mouth as to say something, but closed it after a moment of hesitation, spun on his heels, and left. The door closed behind him, drowning the room into semi-darkness, the only light entering from the window. Daylight was fading fast already as it always did in the winter, but the few weak rays invading his prison were soothing, like rays of hope breaking through the darkness of their predicament.

He closed his eyes, willing himself to fall asleep, but a soft click from the door made him sit up in surprise. A blonde head popped in the opening, and two startling blue eyes glittered in a round face. His sister, Maja, tiptoed her way in, closing the door quietly behind her.

"Are you awake, Jaali?"

Unfocused eyes searched for him in the dimness, and he felt tempted to pretend he was indeed asleep. But this was his sister—for better or worse—and he owed it to himself to at least see what she had to say.

Swinging his legs over the edge of the bed, Jaali took a few moments before speaking. "I'm awake. What do you want? If you're coming to exorcise the evil from me, don't waste your time."

She flinched, her eyes still searching and adjusting to the lack of light. "I don't think you're evil. You're my brother."

Jaali exhaled, his shoulders relaxing. "Then, why are you here? You joined the mob to go hunt down my wife."

Maja took two more steps closer, her eyes a bit more focused. "I still think she bewitched you." The words crushed him. For a brief moment, he had allowed himself to believe his sister had changed her mind. "They have wicked ways of messing with your mind."

He snorted, bitterness rising in his throat and burning his tongue. "*They*? Who are *they*? The evil slavers who kidnap Fjorden children and sell them into slavery? Is that the *they* you speak of?" He knew exactly who she was referring to, but he wanted to hear it from her own lips. Maybe then he wouldn't feel so guilty about his feelings toward his own flesh and blood.

"The dark *duivels*. All of them." She lowered her voice to almost a whisper, her eyes darting around her in fear. "They have ways of making you do and think what they want. That's how they steal our children. They—" She searched for the word, her teeth biting into her lower lips. "They hypnotize them, steal their willpower, and then convince them to go with them without a fight."

Jaali's insides burned, gathering steam like a tea kettle getting ready to explode. "Is that what you think they do? Do you really believe that those of us who were kidnapped didn't put up a fight? That we went willingly, under some kind of trance?" He fought with the urge to yell out.

"It would explain why we can never catch them in the act. How we never hear any of the children cry or scream."

"So you come up with a cockamamie idea that we must have gone willingly?" Jaali couldn't believe his own ears. It was as if his sister was blaming his kidnapping on him being softheaded. "Did it ever occur to you that they gagged us so we couldn't scream? That our small children's strength was not a match to the kidnappers', being fully grown, strong men and women?" His breathing had become shallow, anger and disbelief bubbling up to the surface like hot lava. "We fought. We fought with all the strength of our little bodies. So fiercely we had bruises and sore muscles afterward to prove it. Some of us twisted limbs or even broke an arm trying to break free from the Mabaya warriors. But they were many and strong. We were one and little."

There was silence, Maja lowering her gaze to her hands. Jaali tried to control his heart and his lungs, coax them into slowing down. There was no point in losing it now and giving his people more reason to think he was under some kind of spell.

"Our houses are small." Maja lifted his eyes, hard as stones and just as cold. "We would have heard something. No, we know the dark *duivels* put a hex on you. And now that *duivel* you married is doing it again—making you think you love her and that she's a good person when in fact she's here to put a spell on all of us, get us ready for the plucking. Take away what's ours."

Jaali sprang to his feet, propelled by an anger he had never felt before. He had hated his owner and his friends who had turned him into their play toy and couldn't care less how much they hurt him—physically and emotionally. But they were strangers to him, people he had no reason to care about. This was his family, his people. This was a special kind of anger. It didn't come from hate but from a sense of utter betrayal.

"Why do you hate me so much?" The words spilled out

of his mouth before he had a chance to stop them. "I'm your brother. Your only brother. Why aren't you glad I'm back?"

Maja's eyes burnt a hole in his. "Do you think it was easy to be the one who was left behind?" Jaali blinked in surprise. "After they took you, *Mamma* couldn't pull herself together, and *Pappa* spent his whole energy and time trying to make her happy." Her usually pretty face contorted into a frown and tears twinkled in her eyes.

"You say that as if it was my fault," Jaali said, his mind still reeling from the anger his sister projected.

"I was left to my own devices, Jaali." Her voice had softened a little, emotion making her stutter as she spoke. "No one to tuck me in at night. No one to read me a bedtime story. Things got better after Elin was born, but it didn't last long." He had a sister he had never met. Jaali's heart bled a little more.

Hardness returned to Maja's voice. "Your wife's people came back, not even three years later, and took her away too. *Mamma* never recovered—"

Jaali made a move to comfort her, but she flinched away. "Sorry, Maja. I didn't know we had another sister. I'm so glad you were fortunate enough not to be kidnapped along with the two of us."

The daggers in his sister's eyes punctured his heart and soul. "Fortunate? You think I was fortunate to be left without the attention and care of my parents? The one who nobody wanted, not even the slavers." She wiped the unshed tears with the back of her hand and laughed bitterly. "You and Elin made me feel guilty for being left behind.

And then miserable because you took the love of my parents with you. They didn't care I was their daughter and needed them to love me. All they could think about was their lost children."

"I'm so sorry that you felt that way, but our parents loved you, I'm sure. They were just heartbroken." For the first time, Jaali's heart went out to his sister.

"Don't be sorry for me, *bror*. I did well with my life." She spat the words. "I have a good husband and wonderful children. But you come back to try and take what's rightfully mine. Again."

Jaali was puzzled. What was she talking about?

"You came back just in time to claim our father's inheritance, to insinuate yourself back into his heart so that he leaves me out in the cold again. He'll forget who was here with him throughout *Mamma*'s illness, and who held his hand after she died. All because one of his favorite children has come back. That's why I hate you."

Jaali couldn't handle any more of this woman's misplaced anger. "Leave. Now!" His voice, still quiet, left no doubt as to the seething wrath threatening to burst out of him. "Leave before I do something I'll forever regret. Leave."

Maja huffed, visibly annoyed by his reaction, but did as he asked. One minute she was standing in front of him, the next she was gone. He stood frozen, afraid that if he moved his heart would crack just a little more. So much for the dreams he had for years, first as a child laborer in the furniture factory, and then at the hands of the slaver that broke him inside and out—a million tiny pieces that

Milenda had helped him put together again. The same princess his people wanted dead and gone. Dreams of rejoining his family, being part of the unit they once were—loved and cherished. Instead, his mother was dead, his sister convinced he was not in his right mind, and a father still absent somewhere. Who knew how he would react when he came back in the spring? Jaali had no intentions of waiting around to find out. He had escaped the *Jangwa Pori,* these walls were not going to hold him for long.

"I'm coming, *msichana*. I'm coming soon."

FREYA'S WARNING

From that spot, the icy world of *Isvärld* seemed distant and untouchable. Perched on top of a rock that protruded from the ledge that had become her home for the past few days, Milenda scanned the snow-blanketed land beneath her. The soft white waves on the ground, miles below, lent the world a tone of ethereal beauty and purity. If she didn't know better, she could well believe evil had left those shores for good. Mother Nature was very good at atoning for human flaws with its miraculous and never-ending wonders. The princess sighed, her heart half singing in joy, the other half in sadness. She missed her husband, she missed what she had never had—peace and domestic bliss.

Behind her, Mjusi had joined the younger wyverns in a mad chase around Mama Msitu, who curled around herself like a giant cat, her massive tail under her muzzle. The large creature mirrored the calm most mothers showed around their young ones. Would Milenda ever experience that with her own children? Or would her heirs suffer from the same lack of stability and safety she and Jaali never seemed to get rid of?

She turned her eyes back to the expanse at the foot of the mountain, majestic and peaceful. Milenda took a deep breath and wished nature would fill her with that same peace. A loud boom of wings made her turn around. Tausi was back, landing with such grace it was hard to believe he was as big as he was. From his jaws, two animals hung, obviously dead. It would be dinner later. Milenda was now used to the pattern. The male wyvern left every morning, flying upward but never down, and returning later with prey. At first, Milenda had thought they would have to eat their food raw like Mjusi often did, but was astounded when Mama Msitu burned the pelts and cooked the meat underneath the hides with her fiery breath.

While the young dragons gathered around their father, bickering and making clicking sounds with their tongues, Mjusi came to sit by her. He took a look at the view and, throwing his head back, yowled—a deep, heart-wrenching wail that reflected all what she had inside her heart: yearning, pain, and love. She wrapped her arms around his neck and rested her face against his scaly skin.

"I love you, my friend."

Life had settled into a quiet, easy routine. Being with the wyverns on top of that mountain was ironically the most tranquil time she had had in recent months, despite being separated from Jaali. He visited almost every night, once the others in the village were asleep in their beds, and they found a measure of solace in each other's arms. But as morning approached, the glittery magic of their encounters faded to black and Jaali had to return to his lonely room in town. Parting was never easy. Even though connected in ways no one else was, there was always that nagging fear that the link may one day break and leave them on their own.

"Will you stop being scared of what's never going to happen?" The voice yanked her out of her reverie. Freya stood to her side, magnificent in the most inappropriate clothes for the climate, her hands on her small waist and a frown on her ivory face. "Your gift is a birthright. You'll die with it, like it or not."

Milenda turned her body around to face the demigoddess. "But what if something happens to Jaali? When he was shot in the desert, I lost contact with him. I couldn't find him."

"You won't need to find him if he's dead." The bluntness of Freya's words hit Milenda with the force of a punch.

"I don't know how it works in the world of the gods, but humans need those they love even after they die." It came out louder and harder than she thought wise, but who did this goddess think she was to discount her love for her husband as something disposable? "You may not put any value on love, but I do."

The beautiful woman was unaffected by Milenda's angry words. She patted Mjusi, who closed his eyes and purred like a feline. *Traitor.*

"Don't be such a child. Of course, I put value in love, but you're a queen—or you will be. As such you must sometimes be practical. A dead husband won't give you the heirs you need. Shed your tears and move on." Freya's almost petulant tone made Milenda's blood boil. What did she know about love? Milenda knew the stories about her and her many lovers—use them and discard them. "Don't let your love for any man cloud your judgment."

"My love for Jaali doesn't cloud my judgment," Milenda said in spite of her resolve not to react. "In fact, it clears things for me. It makes me strong and willing to fight for whatever I must fight for. It makes me a better person, and it will make me a better queen. He's the voice I hear when I'm in doubt and the force that propels me into action. There's no confusion, no bad judgment."

The goddess's eyes turned briefly to the princess. *Is that a look of respect?* No, she must have dreamed it. Freya returned to her petting.

"I'm glad to hear. You'll need all your wits in the months to come." That sounded ominous. What did she mean by that? "In the meantime, we have to come up with a plan to get that man of yours out of prison."

Finally, something Milenda was excited to hear. With Freya's help, they actually stood a chance. Jaali thought at first that he could just never return to town after one of his nightly visits, but Milenda was sure that couldn't be done. She remembered Asha telling her how her body was still in her royal room while she reached out to Jaali in the desert. Which meant part of them was left behind every time she reached out, and leaving part of yourself behind was not an option.

"What are we going to do then?" The little seed of hope from the goddess's words was already taking root and beginning to grow in her heart. "What's the plan?"

Freya looked at her, an amused half smile on her lips. "Calm down, child. This has to be well planned, and good plans take some time." Coming from a goddess, that was not reassuring. Since deities didn't seem to have a sense of time, "some time" could mean years. Milenda and Jaali didn't have years.

"I can't possibly stay up here with the *msitus* forever, can I?" Aware she sounded like a moody adolescent, Milenda lowered her eyes and bit her lip.

"It's warm here and you have plenty of food, not to mention protection." Her logic was sound, but the heart was not so reasonable. "Your man comes almost every night and pleasures you." Milenda's *matangazos* burnt in embarrassment. How did she know that? Had she been watching them all this time? "It looks like a good life to me."

She might as well say it. "There is more to life than food and sex, Freya, and I want it all."

For the second time, Milenda thought she spied a twinkle of respect in the goddess's eye. "Good. That's the right attitude for a good queen."

Freya adjusted the strip of cloth covering her generous breasts and held her lower lips between her teeth. The silence grew and became almost palpable between them. Milenda squirmed on the rock where she sat, her eyes firmly glued to the beautiful woman beside Mjusi.

"I'm thinking we may have to teach the villagers a lesson," Freya said suddenly, her eyes still distant and glazed. Milenda was not sure she was talking to her or just thinking out loud. "And our wyvern friends may be just the ones to do it."

The wyverns? What exactly was Freya planning? Milenda had quickly learned that the creatures never went down that mountain. When they flew, it was always up, as if they avoided the valley at all costs. She was reminded of what Karlsson had said about dragons—that they were dangerous and had not been seen at all in centuries. For what Milenda could tell so far, they would—not unlike human families—certainly defend themselves and their own if necessary, but otherwise, they were peace-loving creatures who wouldn't hurt anyone by choice.

Milenda was about to ask about her plans when Freya's head snapped up as if finally freed from whatever thoughts she was buried in. "I'll come up with something brilliant. I always do." *How modest of her*. "In the meantime, you keep doing what you're doing—especially what you're doing with your Fjorden man. I have to try some of that." With a wink that made Milenda's *matangazos* burn brightly again, the goddess wavered and vanished like smoke in the wind.

Still burning from Freya's comments and the idea that she had been watching their lovemaking, Milenda stood up and headed to her cave, closely followed by Mjusi, who had been napping under the goddess's oddly tender ministrations. What was the deity planning? It should make her happy and hopeful to know a creature of such power was helping them, but instead, it gave her pause. Gods were well known for their volatility, and she was not ready to totally trust that Freya was doing all of this for their benefit. The little nagging doubt that she may be serving some less altruistic purposes was ever present in Milenda's mind.

"You trust her, don't you, Mjusi?" The *msitu* threw her a sideways glance as they ducked inside the cave. "I always trust your judgment, but in this case, are you sure we can trust Freya?"

Milenda busied herself folding her blankets and placing them against the wall. She didn't have much with her, but she still enjoyed a tidy space. When Jaali came to her at night, she wanted him to feel at home somehow. With tenderness, she swiped a hand over the *nguba*, her wedding blanket. The one thing Jaali had selfishly kept through his years in indenture as a reminder of his family and home until he offered it to her—a symbol of his wish to forever keep her safe and loved. That blanket was the only thing they had been wearing when they were taken from the room on their wedding night and carried to the ship they were to sail North. Her beloved *nguba* that she had stuffed in her bag, before food or weapons, to carry in her escape.

With her back against the wall, the princess dropped to the ground and stared out the cave opening. The days were longer now, and night had to struggle harder to make its daily appearance. Spring was coming. The day before, Milenda had found a small flower, white with purplish highlights, growing in a patch of newly sprung grass. It was different from anything she had ever seen in Afrika, and the temptation to pick it and place it between the kinks of her hair had been strong, but in the end, she thought better. It was the first sign of spring, heralding the end of the snowy season and the return of Jaali's father.

Jaali's father held a special place in her heart. Milenda had never met him of course, but even though she would never admit this to anyone, she had an irrational hope that he would be the one to open his arms and welcome both her husband and her. She knew she was being childish and most likely heading for a big heartbreak, but she needed to latch on to something. Her father had changed, hadn't he? When she least expected it, he surprised her by being the father she had always wanted him to be and ultimately the one to save her and Jaali. So why couldn't her father-in-law change the way things were? Why was it so hard to believe he may truly love and accept them as they were?

Milenda leaned her head against the rock wall and closed her eyes, the *nguba* bunched up against her chest, and Mjusi lying beside her. Was it too juvenile of her to say a prayer to Yemanjá and ask for a miracle of sorts? The demigoddess had already given her so much, was it fair—or wise—for her to ask yet another favor?

Scrunching her eyes, she decided it was well worth the risk. "Mother of all things, hear my prayer. Make Jaali's father pliant to our needs, sympathetic to our situation. Let him be our ally. For Jaali who has been alone most of his life without the love of his family. Give him this. Please, Mother, give him *something*."

It was quiet outside. The wyverns were most likely

napping in the tepid warmth of the sleepy sun. The world had gone silent. Milenda was not sure whether she dreamed or actually heard it—a female voice from afar, chuckling and clucking like Mama Nyeusi used to do. "Silly girl. Did you think we brought you this far just to let you and your pale man die?"

***

JAALI

Something had happened. The villagers had been gathering in quiet clusters outside his window, the hush-hush of their voices reaching his ears indecipherable through the thick glass. That morning, when the sun was still just a threat in the sky, Lara had brought him his food, her eyes unusually lowered, and hurried out the door. Jaali strained his neck, looking for some explanation to their strange behavior but couldn't find any. The groups of people came and went, leaving their footsteps in the thinning snow cover on the ground.

Frustrated and a little worried, Jaali sat on his cot, wanting to reach out to Milenda again but afraid someone would come through the door at any moment. He had been with her the night before. Memories of how she felt beneath him, as he covered her silky skin in kisses, flooded his mind so vividly, his body immediately reacted.

Worried that a villager would come in and surprise him in a state reserved for Milenda's eyes only, Jaali stretched on top of the cot, his back to the door, and willed the memories away. They kept coming, one after another—the way her small breasts fit perfectly in the palm of his hand, her flavor on his tongue, her heat against his, how they fit together like two pieces of a puzzle. *Not the right place or time.* With a deep breath, Jaali tried to block his own thoughts, his own desire. All in vain. He needed his wife there with him.

"Well, she can't be here with you right now, young Fjorden, so you might as well pleasure yourself." The voice was more effective than a dip in the snow. Propelled by some inner coil, Jaali jumped off the bed to stand facing the most beautiful woman he had ever seen. An almost naked woman, her long blonde hair falling in cascades over her barely covered breasts. *Freya?*

The woman scanned him from head to toe, taking her sweet time and pausing along the way with a little *mmm* of approval. Jaali felt quite naked under her scrutiny, even though he was covered in thick winter clothes.

"Who can blame her for giving up on her throne when she can have you instead?" Freya—for he was quite certain now it was her—grazed her hand across her lips suggestively.

Jaali cringed. He had seen that look before many times, and it was not one he missed or wanted to be reminded of. "Freya? What can I do to help you?" As soon as he said it, he remembered the stories his people used to whisper by the fire when they thought the children were asleep. The stories about their sex-hungry goddess who often took lovers from the mortal world. "Is something wrong with Milenda?" Was that why the villagers were acting so oddly?

The goddess stretched and shook her head, her eyes still trained on Jaali's body. "Gods no. Yemanjá would have me for dinner if I let anything happen to her mortal protégé. I just thought I would come and feast my eyes on the man who keeps her so… pleased."

Nausea overtook him. *No, no.* He had put all of this behind him. His demons. His past. This deity was bringing all those awful feelings back to the surface with her hungry eyes and sexual innuendo.

"Stop shaking like that. I'm not going to ravish you. Relax." Freya looked somewhere between amused and annoyed. "You're a sweet piece of mortal flesh, but that's not why I'm here." Her voice changed. The seductress was no longer there. "I visited your neighbors last night."

Still trying to get his trembling under control, Jaali made himself stare into the woman's eyes. "Visited? What do you mean?"

"Let's just say, they all had the same dream." That would explain all the whispers and haunted looks. "In the dream, I told them they better think things over in what concerns you and your Afrikan princess."

Should he even ask? "Or what?"

"Or bad things may start happening." Milenda had told him about Yemanjá's cryptic talk. Apparently, it was a goddess's habit. "Don't get scared. Nothing really bad is going to happen, but they'll be terrified."

"What shall I do?" He was tempted to thank her, but that validated the idea that he owed her something. Jaali didn't want to owe this goddess anything.

"You just rest your pretty body and let their panic do the rest." She yawned as if growing tired of the conversation. "Just enjoy the show. I'll be watching too. Goodbye, young Fjorden." And she was no longer there.

He had no idea what she meant, but he was glad to see her gone. His body was still shaking from the unsettling feelings the goddess's words and lascivious glares had unearthed. It had been a while since he had felt so soiled, so unworthy of his wife's love. He cursed Freya under his breath and repeated Milenda's words to himself like a mantra, "I am worthy. I am worthy."

After a few minutes of slow breathing, he felt calmer. *Did Freya say she was pressuring the villagers into letting me go?* For the first time since the goddess had entered his room, he could breathe easily, a new hope lighting a little flame in his heart. He had no idea how Freya was planning on accomplishing that—and he was probably better off not knowing—but it was something to look forward to, to hold on to.

The door opened and Arvid and another man he had seen on another occasion walked in, eyes still glued to the ground, as if suddenly the bare wooden floor of the room was of extremely interest. They closed the door behind them and stopped shy of his cot where Jaali sat, hands by his side and eyes glaring at the two men.

"The council met." Arvid's deep, low voice reverberated through the mostly empty space. "To decide what to do with you."

Jaali waited for a few seconds, but neither men

volunteered an explanation. "Well? What did you decide?"

The other man cleared his throat and raised his eyes to him for the first time. "It was decided that we need more time to make a final decision."

What does that even mean? "You decided that you didn't want to decide?" Jaali couldn't hold back the sarcasm from his voice.

"We need more time." Arvid hooked his thick thumbs into the loops of his belt, his legs apart as if trying to find balance on a moving ship. "We haven't found your *duivel,* and we're not sure about you, being under the spell like you are."

Jaali's sigh came out louder than he'd expected it. "For the millionth time, I am not under any spell. My wife is not a *duivel* or a witch." Why was he trying? It was a waste of his time. "If you haven't decided, why are you here?"

"To tell you we're not going to hurt you. We're in talks with a *Seiðmenn.*" So, the goddess had scared them indeed if they were calling on a *seidr* expert, one of the oldest traditional magic and spiritual practices in the Northern Lands. Not scared enough to change their minds, but just enough to make them feel the need to be on Jaali's good side and find outside help. "We don't want you to think we'd hurt you in any way."

"You must be desperate if you're calling on an unmanly one, an *ergi* to help you." The others cringed. Traditionally, men who practiced the *seidr*, a magic tradition followed mainly by women, were not well respected by the population at large. But they were feared for their powers. "Right, so that's it?" The two men nodded. Jaali threw himself down on the bed and rolled to the other side. "Goodnight then. You know where the door is."

There was silence for a few seconds and then the shuffle of steps moving away, shortly followed by a door opening and closing. He was alone again. He turned around to peek out the window. There was still a faint thread of light coming from outside. He wondered whether it would be safe to reach out to Milenda right away, but decided to wait until the full cover of night had fallen.

After arguing about the villagers' misconceptions about what or who Milenda was for over a month, he had given up. His mouth would still utter the words every time anyone came to visit, but in his heart the fight was gone. He went through the motions during the day: eating, sleeping, washing up as much as he could in the tiny bathroom of the prison, sleeping some more.

It was at night that life returned, when his heart resumed its beating and hope and excitement surged through his veins all over again. The thought of seeing his wife, holding her in his arms, was a powerful motivator to let go of any doubts, any fears, any of the blues that assailed him throughout the day as he sat alone in that room with nothing to do.

It was not that he couldn't live without Milenda. He just didn't want to. His jewel made his life brighter, colorful, full of promise—the exact things he had been missing his whole life. When he closed his eyes, he could see her face, eyes sparkling like emeralds nestled in her beautiful amber skin and framed by her unruly black hair. Her *matangazos* burning as he grazed his fingers along her neck and shoulder. It made him glow thinking about her, a warm feeling that started in his heart and quickly spread to all parts of his body.

Night had arrived, and he couldn't wait any longer. With his mind, he felt his way to where Milenda was, asking for permission to enter. The door was open as usual. Milenda welcomed him with an open mind.

"I thought you'd never come." Milenda had stopped reaching out for fear of witnesses and had to wait for him to do it. His princess stood, her arms crossed across her chest, a foot tapping on the dirt floor, and her lips pinched. He smiled.

"I was waiting for darkness. I had a lot of visitors today." Well, more than usual anyway. "Freya is causing a stir among the villagers."

Milenda's eyes widen. "Freya? What did she do? She came to visit me again a couple of days ago."

Jaali hesitated for a moment and then recounted his encounter with the demigoddess. He left out the part about how the deity's words had reawakened his demons, his fears. She would have understood, but he didn't want to give her any more to worry about. Or, knowing Milenda, give her any reason to hate the one person who could help them.

"What do you think she's going to do?" Milenda bit her lower lip and the heat she always ignited in him flared. "She mentioned something about the wyverns being the ones to do it, but she didn't go into details."

Distracted by the way she wrapped a strand of her hair around her finger, Jaali almost missed her last words. "Wyverns? She's going to use them to do… well, whatever it is she's planning on doing?"

She dropped the hair and scooted closer to Jaali, their backs against the wall of the cave. The dragons were all asleep in their caves except Mjusi, who in spite of his new family still slept close to Milenda—Jaali was not sure whether to protect her or because Milenda had always been the only family he knew. His dark green shape, all curled up upon itself, laid just a few feet away from them. Jaali could hear the creature's peaceful breathing in the silence of the cave.

The sparse furnishings gave the space a certain air of emptiness, but Jaali loved it here. It was warmer than his cell and quiet in a different way, a friendlier way. In town, the silence was permeated with the hate and fear of the villagers. Here nothing stained the stillness of the night.

"I just hope that whatever she does won't hurt anyone. She doesn't strike me as a merciful goddess." Milenda leaned her head against his shoulder and her hair tickled his face. Her voice quivered a little when she spoke again. "You know she's watched us make love."

Jaali turned to look at her. "What? Not that I'm surprised, but…" Not after what she had managed to do to his confidence earlier that day. "How dare she?"

Milenda giggled, brushing his face with her fingers. "*Wimbo wa moyo*, she's a goddess."

Until he had met Milenda, gods were mere characters in

textbooks and stories. Now he was having uncomfortable conversations with them. Still, it annoyed him to no end that Freya thought it perfectly acceptable to spy on them when they were intimate.

His princess lifted her eyes to him, and his anger dissolved into nothing. He could get lost in the forest of her eyes shining in the moonlight. Jaali held her waist and pulled her onto his lap, burying his lips in the crook of her honey-flavored neck. Milenda's fingers interlaced behind his head and pulled him closer with a soft groan.

"Since Freya is such a fan of watching us love each other, let's give her something to talk about." Jaali crushed his lips against hers, prying them open with his tongue, and reveled in her taste. It was never enough.

Milenda grasped his thick woolen sweater and pulled it over his head, taking his undershirt along with it. She caressed him across the chest in a fluttering of fingers and hungry lips. It didn't take long until their clothes had been strewed around the dirt floor of the cave and they stood naked, skin to skin, shaking in anticipation. His princess's *matangazos* shone brightly, their light joining the moonbeams to illuminate the space with a warm glow.

Gently, Jaali turned Milenda around, lifted her up, and guided her to his lap. He slid inside her, her warmth enveloping and caressing him whole, and moaned. Milenda moved on top of him like the ocean tide, ebbing and flowing, small whimpers of pleasure escaping her lips. His hands circled around her and cupped her breasts, planting kisses along her back and raising his hips to meet her. Jaali felt her quake in his arms as she reached her climax, and he gave himself permission to let it go, to lose his seed inside his wife. Connected. Whole.

Later, when Milenda slept peacefully within the protection of his arms, Jaali smiled at no one in particular. Freya had brought back feelings he'd rather forget, but his wife's love had erased them again, obliterated them as if they were mere specks of dust. Milenda's love was the antidote to the poison the goddess had fed him earlier.

"You cannot separate something that is one, Freya. Not even gods can break something as elemental as our love apart."

THE WYVERNS

Milenda

A cold nose woke her up, nudging her face with such insistence all her internal alarms were raised. Milenda sat up, her head swimming slightly from the sudden movement, and glanced at her winged friend.

"What's going on, Mjusi?"

She scratched her head and found a small stick stuck to her hair. With her fingers, she attempted at combing her uncooperative hair into submission. She missed Asha, her young girl servant, who patiently would put a comb through that thick hair of hers and always seemed to be able to coax it into fitting snuggly and obediently under an *ibhayi*, the turban-style hat women wore in Natale. She giggled a little, thinking of what the villagers would think of the elaborate *geles* she was made to wear for formal events, some voluminous enough to make her look a couple feet taller.

Mjusi was still begging for her attention, scratching on the floor, shaking his head in an agitated way and growling.

She crawled to him and wrapped her hands around his neck, trying to calm him down. "What is it?"

The *msitu* pulled in the direction of the cave's entrance, and she followed, grabbing her coat on the way out. The days were getting longer and warmer, but the mornings still carried an extra chill. Milenda exited the cave right behind Mjusi, stretching her arms above her head and shaking the last kinks of sleep off her body. The wyvern family was gathered by the giant rock Milenda had come to think of as a table since the creatures seemed to favor that spot for their meals. They all seem slightly agitated, the funny little clicking sounds they made when anxious echoing in the air.

As she neared the dragons, they pulled apart, revealing a familiar—and not always welcomed—figure in the middle. *Freya! What is she doing here?* Even though the demigoddess had never done anything wrong, Milenda had come to think of her as trouble. It was obvious Freya was not too worried about what or how her human charges felt or about their well-being. While Yemanjá showed some genuine concern and love for her creatures, this Fjorden deity showed no such care. It scared Milenda a bit. Jaali seemed even less keen about accepting the goddess's help.

"It's about time you woke up, Princess." Freya's tone of voice rang somewhere between sarcastic and playful. "I thought you were going to sleep all day."

Milenda could play the game. "What do we owe the rare pleasure of your visit, Freya?"

The goddess gave her a look of appraisal, her lips stretching into a grin. "Glad to see that royal streak coming out." The wyverns lingered around her, still chattering to each other in a cacophony of clicks and squeaks. "I came to give our wyvern friends instructions."

Milenda's hackles rose. Mjusi was her friend, and she wouldn't take it lightly if Freya was messing with his safety.

"Do you ever stop fretting?" The goddess's blue eyes narrowed to a slit as she crossed her arms in front of her. "I wouldn't hurt these creatures. But I do have something I need them to do for me. And for you, ungrateful child."

The burn from her *matangazos* made Milenda shift on her feet, her eyes averting from the magnificent woman facing her. "Sorry, Freya. They are so… nervous, I thought that maybe—"

"Maybe the coldhearted goddess was just sending them to certain doom?" The sarcasm was back in her voice. She pointed at the wyverns and lowered her voice to a whisper. "You don't know me, so don't judge me, young woman."

Properly ashamed for her misjudgment of the goddess, Milenda stared at her own feet. "You're right. I, of all people, should know better than to judge someone I don't know well."

Freya's cackle made Milenda snap her head up. "I don't get offended easily, Princess. Don't make the mistake of thinking I'm kindhearted, because I'm not. I may not be a bleeding heart like your Yemanjá, but I do care for my children. My way." She laughed again, throwing her head backward, her almost-white hair flying in waves around her face.

Mjusi stared at the goddess with a funny tilt of the head, and Milenda laughed under her breath. She wasn't the only one who thought Freya was strange.

"The wyverns will fly into town tomorrow and scare those fools into compliance." Her laughter gone, the goddess's eyes hardened. "They haven't made an appearance in a couple hundred years. I think it's time we remind the mortals who rules the land."

Outrage bubbled up Milenda's throat. "Mama Msitu and Tausi are obviously not happy with the idea." She pointed at the two large creatures still clicking at each other.

Freya reached out to the female wyvern and patted her neck. "They're nervous because they fear they'll be hunted again like they were a long time ago."

"And you're still sending them? What if their fears are right?" Milenda's voice rose in spite of her attempt at keeping calm. "They wanted me dead because they thought I was a witch. They will do the same with the *msitus* out of fear."

"Your loyalty to these creatures is commendable but unnecessary. I will protect them." The finality in her voice prevented Milenda from further questioning the idea's merit. She didn't want anything to happen to these gentle creatures who had so generously welcomed her among them—Mjusi's long-lost family, the only family he had. She knew how hard it was growing up without a mother, a sibling, a father who noticed she was alive. It wouldn't be fair to take that away from her friend.

Freya turned her attention to the dragons. "Tomorrow at first light, you swoop down the village and melt some snow with your breath. They won't be armed because they don't expect an attack. I'll do the rest." The creatures nodded their heads. "Leave the fledglings with the princess."

Without as much as a goodbye, the goddess disappeared, leaving only her footsteps on the snow as witness to her presence there. Milenda watched as the adult wyverns walked away, their heads together, their children following close behind. Mjusi rubbed his head against her legs, and she hoped Freya was right—that nothing bad would happen to the magnificent creatures who had been her friendly hosts for the past month or so.

"They'll be all right," Milenda said more to herself than Mjusi. "Freya will take care of them." Her friend looked up at her again with an expression that she could only describe as skeptical. She laughed. "Really. I think deep down inside she does care about your family." At least, Milenda hoped she did.

She hadn't eaten anything yet, but her stomach churned and rumbled as if she had eaten rotten eggs. Grabbing a container, she rushed to the corner where the snow was always miraculously unfrozen and dipped it in for a drink. It didn't help. The stress of listening to the troublesome goddess making equally worrisome plans for her friends had turned her insides to mush. She heaved and bile burned its way up her throat. *No, no. I can't get sick now.* She was stronger than that. She had survived the emotional roller coaster of the Trials, she was not about to let a little stress undo her.

Mjusi cooed, his head bumping into her side. "I'll be all right. Freya got me all in knots." Bent over herself, her arms across her stomach, the princess allowed the waves of nausea to ride their way through her. Eventually, and as suddenly as it'd started, it subsided. Milenda was able to stand straight again.

"What's that?" she asked the *msitu* who had gone to fetch something and now held it in his muzzle in offering. The bloodied rodent that Mjusi so generously was offering her caused a new surge of nausea. She rushed to a corner and emptied the meager contents of her stomach over the edge.

Afraid she would throw up again, Milenda made her way back to the cave and curled up on her blankets, holding her stomach and praying silently to Yemanjá. Without realizing, she must have reached out to her husband, because before she could do anything about it, she was in his room, curled up on the small cot.

"*Msichana*, what are you doing here?" Jaali exclaimed, as she groaned in both pain and dismay. "Are you sick?" He ran to her side, kneeling beside the bed, his hand checking her forehead. "What's wrong?"

Fighting another wave of nausea, Milenda tried to straighten up and pretend she was well. Her body wouldn't let her. "I'm all right. Just nauseated. Freya—"

"Hell, what did she do now? Did she hurt you?" Jaali was still checking her for possible injuries.

"No. Just the stress she always seems to cause. I think it just upset my stomach." The nausea came and went, making her dry heave. "Sorry, Jaali."

"What are you sorry for? Not feeling well? I think you saw me in much worse shape before." They giggled at the bittersweet reminder. Then it had not been amusing. And it had happened way too often. From injuries to fevers, they had gone through hell together. They could do it again.

Jaali sat on the edge of the cot and cradled her, rocking her gently in his arms. The warmth of his body against hers was soothing, and she began feeling better. Her eyes, heavy as lead, began to close. "I'm so tired."

"*Msichana*, you can't stay here. It's dangerous. Lara will be coming soon with food and if she sees you…."

Reluctantly, Milenda swung her legs over the edge and sat, staring into her favorite sight: Jaali's eyes, so blue, so translucent. She could see herself reflected in them, and if she looked closer, she could see eternity. "*Wimbo wa moyo*, you're right. I need to go." Jaali moved forward to kiss her, but she pulled back with a giggle. "I just threw up. Trust me. You don't want to kiss me."

Jaali touched her forehead with his and laughed softly. "You'll always taste sweet to me." He planted a kiss on her lips as if to prove it, and Milenda opened her eyes to the cave in the mountain. She took her fingers to where her skin still tingled from her husband's lips and sighed. Her stomach was still unsettled and empty, but her heart was full.

* * *

JAALI

At first, he thought he was dreaming. The sound of screams mixed and mingled with loud swooshes and what sounded like the crackling of fire. Jaali had been awake for a while, lying back on his cot and revisiting his night with Milenda. He turned his head toward the window. Day was in full bloom, but there were flashes of shadow behind the glass. He got up and rushed to the window.

Outside there was chaos. People ran in every direction, hands in the air, screaming in terror. The shadows he had seen became more ominous as they flew over the whiteness of the land, grazing the top of the trees. The wyverns!

Freya had not been lying. The two adult dragons were wreaking havoc in town. As far as he could tell from his tiny window, nothing had been destroyed. A couple small abandoned buildings on the outskirts of town were burning to the ground, but nothing else seemed touched. After a couple of minutes of swooping down over the town and its inhabitants, the creatures flew away.

The villagers had all taken refuge inside their houses. Jaali didn't know whether this had been a good move to help them or if Freya in her efforts to rescue them had made a serious mistake. The goddess seemed to take human nature for granted, but humans were not as predictable as she thought they were. He had ample experience with that and had learned never to assume people would react a certain way.

Not an hour had passed when the door opened, daylight refreshing the stale air in the room for a few seconds. Arvid led a group of three villagers, which included his sister, her blonde braids in disarray. They all placed themselves in a semicircle around the cot as Jaali sat up to greet them.

"Were those wyverns?" Jaali asked, knowing all too well the answer. He scanned his visitors' faces with curiosity. They were shaken, their faces paler than usual, and a haunted glow in their eyes. "I thought they were a legend."

Arvid cleared his throat, but his voice still wavered. "They haven't been seen in a couple hundred years." There was a hardness to his expression that Jaali hadn't seen there before.

"So, you're going to blame me for this too, right?" He had no doubt that was exactly what the villagers were about to do.

"Not you. Your wife."

Jaali had begun to stand only to fall back onto the bed in surprise. "My wife? Do you think she brought wyverns with her from Natale? Where they don't exist, by the way?" He would keep Mjusi out of the conversation for now. They had never seen him.

"No, but she somehow found a way to awake the ones that had been dormant all these years." The big man looked at the others before continuing. "We've been talking about how to better cut the ties you have with this witch and bring her power over you to an end."

Jaali ran his fingers through his hair, trying not to become angry. "You cannot cut ties that are not there. The only connection I have with my wife is our love and our marriage."

Maja jumped forward, almost excited. "So we cut those ties. The marriage ties."

His glance bounced between Arvid and his sister. Had

he understood that correctly? "You cannot force me into a divorce. Not without her agreeing to it." Could they?

"You were married in another nation, a land of barbarians who don't follow our beliefs. Freya didn't bless it. Odin didn't bless it. It was blessed by the non-gods of the *duivels*. Your marriage is therefore null in the Northern Lands." Maja smirked at him, like a little girl taunting her siblings.

Jaali fought the childish urge to stick his tongue out at her. "If it's true, then why do you say we are still linked? Shouldn't she then be powerless over me?"

Maja squirmed, a grimace on her face. "As long as you believe you're married to the witch, she'll have power over you."

A roll of laughter left his mouth. "So, we're at an impasse then?"

The villagers exchanged a look Jaali didn't like. They had been plotting.

"Klas, the *seiðmenn*, has advised us on what to do." Arvid crossed his massive arms, muscles visible even from beneath the thick winter clothes. "You must marry a local girl."

Jaali jumped to his feet. "What? Marry who? Are you insane? I'm already married."

"Not according to our laws and traditions, dear brother." Maja seemed as if she was enjoying herself, playing this game of cat and mouse. "We have a volunteer from among the single women in town. You'll be married at first light, tomorrow morning."

Taking a couple steps forward, Jaali stopped himself

from attacking his own sister. How could this spiteful, angry woman be his blood relative? He knew that his family had gone through a lot after his kidnapping, but he had managed to keep his human decency and love for others alive even after all the cruelties and indignities the slavers had put him through. Why couldn't this woman have done the same?

"I will not marry anyone." He emphasized each separate word. His heart raced in his chest and it was hard to breathe. "I already have an amazing wife that I love more than life itself. I will not marry anyone else."

Arvid took a step forward and placed a hand on his shoulder. Jaali pulled away. "According to local law, if one or both parties are deemed to be incapable of a rational decision relating to their union, the law keeper, the *genomdrivare*, will have the responsibility to step in and make that decision for them. That means, young Jaali, that I pick a wife for you and for your own good."

Wishing he had his weapon with him, Jaali swung a fist at the big man, but Arvid jumped back just in time to avoid it.

"You have no right." Jaali's heart bled. Once again others were taking control of his life, telling him what to do, not giving him a choice. After a lifetime of indenture, he had thought he had finally freed himself from slavery, but here he was again being enslaved in body and spirit. And this time by his own people. "You have no right." He felt tears pooling in his eyes and anger, hot as magma, collecting inside of him.

"We'll leave you now, but will be back later with your

bride," Maja said, the same ugly smirk still on her face. "I think you'll like her once you get to know her."

Before they could run, Jaali grabbed a bowl from the nearby table and threw it at the small group, hitting Arvid on the chest. "Don't come back. I'll sooner die here alone than marry one of you."

Arvid turned around, anger in his eyes, and bending down he picked up the bowl. "It is all for your own good. You'll thank me later."

Almost hyperventilating, Jaali snarled. "That's what my owner used to say to me. I'll never, ever thank you for this. Get out!"

With the three of them gone, Jaali threw himself on top of the bed, face buried in the pillow and cried—tears of anger and frustration, pain and yearning for the freedom he had earned and now lost again.

"The fools!" Freya was standing in the middle of the room, red faced with a frown. "They don't know what's good for them."

Jaali's anger boiled over. Springing to his feet, he took a few steps until he was close enough to feel the goddess's body heat. She was tall but so was he. He was glad her face was leveled with his because Jaali wanted her to see the wrath in his eyes. "You did this! You're supposed to be helping us, but you made things worse." Spittle flew out of his mouth. Freya didn't flinch. "Now they want to break this spell with another wedding. Do you hear me? They are going to force me to marry a local woman because they think Milenda sicced those dragons on them."

Freya cackled, and for a moment he saw an old hag instead of the beautiful young woman the goddess was. There was a weariness to the set of her lips, the blue of her eyes—the look of someone who had lived many lives and still struggled to understand the world around her. For a moment, a fraction of a second, Jaali was actually sorry for her. Goddess or no goddess, she was a lonely creature who couldn't even control those who worshiped her.

"Young Fjorden, they will obey me. It may take some time, but it will happen." She brushed her fingers across his wet cheek, and he flinched. "I'm a weaver of destiny. Give me the time I need to weave my threads, and they will regret having disobeyed me."

"I don't have time, Freya." Jaali was shaking. "They are marrying me off tomorrow morning. Like the slavers, they will mold me and make me do whatever they want. I don't want to be an indent, a slave again."

Freya's eyes softened, and the sharpness of her tone vanished. "Son of Asker, I promise you this: be strong, be brave, and I will free you from this prison. You'll be happy again."

Jaali tried to hold her and demand an explanation, but his hands met only air. She was gone again. He stood for a while, not sure what to do next. Was there even anything he could do? He was jailed like a criminal between those four walls, and even though he could escape temporarily to be by Milenda's side, he knew he couldn't stay for long. Now, the villagers were going to bring him a sacrificial lamb. It didn't matter she had volunteered—or so they said. She was as much of a pawn in their little power game as he was. It was like the Trials all over again, except this time there was no end in sight. At least not an ending he could look forward to.

How was he going to tell this to his wife? And what would she do? The Jewel was not used to sitting idle while the world fell apart around her. She would want to do something. Anything. But it was too dangerous. He had no doubt the villagers would kill her on sight. They were that afraid of her, of her perceived power.

The hours slugged by, each minute seemingly longer than the one before, until the sun began to fade on the horizon. Peeking through the window, Jaali saw it—a small procession of people coming in the direction of his cell. He wiped his face and pushed the pain and fear to the back of his mind. They wouldn't see him squirm.

The heavy wooden door cracked open and then slowly opened all the way to allow four people in. Arvid came in first, followed by Maja and two unknown people. One, he was guessing, was his bride-to-be. The other, an unfamiliar male, was dressed in layers of strange furs, his blond hair braided into several plaits that stuck in odd directions. They closed the door behind them and approached Jaali on the other side of the room.

"Jaali Asker, we came to present you your bride." Arvid gestured to the young woman behind him to step forward. She was smaller than most adult females in town, and her head and face were partially covered by a colorful scarf. "This is Ebba Bjorgsson. She is very much looking forward to being your wife and clearing you of your connection with the *duivel*."

The use of that word always made him cringe, and he abhorred the fact it was being used in relation to his beloved wife. "Don't call her that," he hissed and fought to stay in control of his anger.

Maja pushed the other woman forward none too gently, and Ebba stumbled forward, her scarf coming undone in the process. Jaali flinched, startled. As the head covering slid off her head, Ebba's small face came into view. The woman was no volunteer—at least not in the full sense of the word.

The skin on her face displayed a devil's mark, a shapeless brownish discoloration that covered the whole right side of her face. A birth defect that had branded her as unwanted by the rest of the population. Jaali remembered her from before. He remembered asking his mother about the young girl in school who covered her face with a scarf and had no friends. As a young boy, he had felt sorry for her, alone and often ridiculed by the other children.

"She was born with the devil's mark," her mom had told him. "Touching her will bring bad luck, so stay away from her."

Jaali had not followed orders. Try as he may, he couldn't abide with the shunning of a child younger than himself. In vain, he tried to start conversations, show her he didn't think she was scary or bad luck. One time he even touched her mark with his fingers, wanting to show her how much he thought the superstition was an old wives' tale. Ebba had not caved in, always withdrawn, alone and weary of all of those around her.

"Ebba, I remember you from school." The girl lifted her brown eyes to him in surprise. "I wish I could say I'm happy to see you, but under the circumstances, I can't."

The young woman flinched and hurried to replace the scarf around her head, her hands fumbling a little. Jaali thought he heard her mumble something, but couldn't be sure.

"You don't have to do this, Ebba," Jaali said, reaching out to touch her arm. She pulled away. "Don't let them bully you into doing something you don't want to do."

Maja laughed—cackled really. The laughter of someone he preferred not to be related to. "Guess what her chances are at getting herself a husband? Marrying you, a handsome, healthy man is a miracle for a deformed little thing like her."

Jaali's eyes hardened, the fire of anger blurring his sight. "Don't call her that!" Ebba stared at him again, her eyes opened wide and unblinking. "There is nothing wrong with you, Ebba. You're different, that's all. Don't let them tell you otherwise." He was familiar with the brainwashing that would cause someone to believe the worst about themselves.

The tiny woman—she was smaller even than Milenda— tilted her head as if studying him. There was doubt, but also a glint of hope in her eyes.

"Stop trying to convince her she's worthy of a normal life." It was his wicked sister again, her face spotted red, pointing at the unfortunate woman. "No one would ever want her. You're a gift from heaven."

In a single move, Jaali stepped in front of Maja, his face close enough to hers he could see her bloodshot eyes.

"If you talk about Ebba that way one more time, I'll forget you're my sister and a woman and show some of the *duivel* ways I learned while in captivity." He spat out his words like a growl and saw Maja flinch. "Do not talk to her like that. You're no better than she is."

Maja took a step back, wiping her hands on her skirts, and stared at the strange man behind them. "Listen to him, all high and mighty. Can you put him in his place, Klas?"

The strange fur-covered man took a step forward and glanced at Jaali, eyes as cold as the snow outside. "Once you marry this woman, the spell you're under will cease to work and you'll see how lucky you are."

"Who the hell are you?" Jaali stepped toward the man, his hands raised.

"I'm Klas Ondhund, the *seiðmenn,* a weaver of destiny." With a silly flourish, the man bowed slightly before him. "Freya has given me the power to choose you a wife."

Laughter bubbled and burst through Jaali's lips. "I doubt that very much." Freya, for once, had nothing to do with this. "I would be very cautious about using Freya's name in a lie. She's not the forgiving kind." The man was ridiculous with odd mannerisms to attract attention to his so-called divine authority. "Go away. I'm not marrying Ebba or anyone else. I'm already married." He looked straight into the young woman's eyes. "Nothing against you, but I love my wife and I'm not going to betray her."

Maja jumped forward, but Arvid, who seemed almost as annoyed with her as Jaali, grabbed her by the arm and pulled her away. "Let's go. We've done what we came for and now it's time to leave." He turned to Jaali. "You will marry Ebba, like it or not. We'll see you tomorrow at first light."

They all turned to leave, except Ebba who stepped closer to him, and before the others could see it or hear it, whispered, "Don't worry. I have a plan."

The woman turned around and moved away so fast, he wasn't sure he hadn't imagined her words. What did she mean? What plan, and for what exactly?

THE ESCAPE

A stream of curses woke her up from a restless dream where Jaali had met a desert *shetani* again. Still sweating, her heart beating a hundred miles a second, Milenda sat up so fast her vision wavered in a stomach-turning motion. Freya was pacing the dirt floor of the cave, hands on her hips, her usual flawless face blotched red.

"Good evening, Your Most Gracious Goddess." Milenda surprised herself with a giggle. Wasn't it strange that she was starting to think of Freya as a regular mortal acquaintance? One you felt comfortable joking around with. "To what do I owe this… pleasure?"

Freya stopped and stared at her, her eyes shooting fire. Milenda knew she probably should be scared, but something about the goddess's demeanor told her the anger was not targeted at her.

"Those ungrateful, stupid, *jävla* weasel subjects of mine!" Milenda cringed at the use of the strong word.

She had heard it a few times on the ship when the sailors thought that if they used Fjorden expletives, she wouldn't understand them, but her ears were still unused to crude language. "I'm going to smite them with fire and brimstone while they sleep."

"You're not really going to do that, are you?" For a moment Milenda was worried for the safety of the villagers. She might not like them, but she did not wish them dead either.

Freya waved a hand above her head. "Probably not. But I will keep my options open." She resumed her pacing, her arms flailing around her like a crazed maestro. "I'm so angry I may decide to weave their destinies in ways they'll wish they were never born."

The princess threw the blanket aside and slowly stood up. Whatever bug she had contracted was still playing havoc with her stomach, and sudden moves didn't help. The familiar churn made her cross her arms over her middle and breathe slowly. "What did they do now?"

"The weasels have hired a *seiðmenn*—and a total inept one—to try and break you and Jaali apart." Milenda straightened up, the flutters in her stomach intensifying. "Instead of following my orders, they thought that they could break the imaginary spell Jaali's under by marrying him off to another woman."

Her heart must have fallen into her stomach, because now Milenda was not only nauseated, but she could feel her frantic heartbeat alongside the flutters. "What? They married him? He's already married." The meager meal she had eaten the night before threatened to spill out. "Can they do that?"

"Not without my blessing. Or Odin's." The goddess had stopped moving, her hands bookending her head. Did demigods have headaches? "I won't give it, of course. And Odin is far too busy with his wars to give a damn about this."

"So what can we do?"

For the first time that morning, the goddess's face lit up in a smile. "You, my dark princess, won't do anything. I will take care of it—somehow." She didn't sound very sure of herself to Milenda. A wave of nausea made Milenda heave. Freya looked at her curiously. "Still sick, then?"

The princess swallowed a big gulp of air, willing the next wave of nausea to win over. "Nerves, all nerves. You focus on Jaali. I'll take care of my stomach."

The goddess did something totally unexpected then. Her hand brushed against Milenda's face in a tender, almost motherly caress as her eyes softened and misted. "You need to rest, child. Let me take care of things. You just take it easy." It was almost as if Yemanjá or Mama Nyeusi were there talking to her instead of this coldhearted goddess. "What does Yemanjá call you? *Kidogo moja*, little one, isn't it? One day you'll do great things, but for now, you must rest."

Stunned into submission, Milenda sat back down in her makeshift bed and took deep, slow breaths to calm herself and her stomach down. "Thank you, Freya. Please, watch over my *wimbo wa moyo*."

"Leave it to me." With a soft poof that sent dirt flying, she was gone.

Milenda slid all the way to the floor and brought her legs up to her chest. What was wrong with her? She had never been, or had to be, nursed back to health. As it turned out, this northern land didn't seem to agree with her at all—hostile people and now nasty virus by the looks of things. She wished she was home, in her beautiful shower house in the palace where she could let the water run over her amid the trees and flowers of the inner courtyard. It was a fanciful wish, for she knew only heartache—and possibly death—waited for her and Jaali in Natale. She sighed and closed her eyes. Maybe if she slept a little longer....

* * *

JAALI

Shortly after sundown, the door opened again. Jaali uttered a quiet thank-you for not having reached out to Milenda early. As anxious as he was to see and share the unsettling news with her, he was afraid the villagers would pay him another visit to make sure he hadn't somehow escaped. Not that he could. Even if he managed to get out of the cabin-turned-prison, where would he go in the middle of the night in subzero temperature?

His eyes tried to adjust to the darkness. The moonlight coming from the window was not enough to illuminate the space. Sitting up quietly, he strained to hear the shuffle of footsteps and the muffled sound of breathing as the door closed again.

"Who's there?" A sudden flash of light startled him, and he brought his hand in front of his eyes. The glare didn't allow him to see clearly yet. "What do you want?"

"I'm here to help." It was the tiny voice of Ebba, her dark silhouette carving an equally small space within the glow of her torch. "I told you I had a plan."

Uncertainty filled his heart. Should he trust this willow of a girl? The one who had volunteered to marry him. The same that all the villagers were holding as their only hope of breaking the spell they believed he was under. "How can I be sure you're telling me the truth? How do I know this is not another trick?"

The young woman approached the bed where he was sitting. As she came closer, he could see a ghost of her face, still half hidden by a woolen scarf, her unusual brown eyes reflecting the glittering light. Jaali's resolve to be on guard collapsed. This woman had been shunned by her own people, isolated, reviled. Not much different than what he had to face after earning his freedom. Worse even in some ways.

"Do you really think I would help those who have treated me like a leper my whole life?" Anger permeated her voice. "Do you believe that I'm that desperate for a husband that I would volunteer to break another marriage apart?"

Jaali sighed. No, he didn't. He couldn't. The girl's situation as an outcast hit too close to home. He knew just how she felt.

"No, I don't believe it, Ebba. But Milenda and I have been betrayed so many times, I have trouble trusting."

Ebba came closer still, and Jaali made room on the bed for her to sit. Hesitating at first, she finally sat down next to him, lit torch in her hands.

"Freya came to us in a dream and warned us that something bad would happen if we didn't let you go." So Freya had been telling the truth. "But these idiots can't see past their hate and fear and thought they could find a compromise. Like you can negotiate with a goddess." Ebba's words dripped with sarcasm and disdain. She didn't think much of her fellow neighbors.

"Forgive me, but what can you do? They obviously don't have much respect for you." Jaali knew she was well aware of it, but still had to be difficult to hear the words. He didn't want to hurt her.

"Yes, that's true. But there is an advantage to being the shunned one—nobody pays any attention to me." As his eyes adapted to the semidarkness, he could see the tiny smile on her lips. She was enjoying this little caper of hers. "Get your things. I'm taking you with me."

"Where to?"

"I'll explain on the way." She stood up and pointed the light across the room, being careful not to point it at the window. "We have to do it under the cover of night. Let's go."

Jaali didn't have much with him, having left most of his possessions in the house he shared with Milenda. In a few minutes, he was ready.

Light extinguished, Ebba unlocked the door and led him across the silent market square. The only light burning was the one in the center of the square, every window drowned in darkness, the moon drawing ghostly shadows in the white snow. Ebba sped through the snow and into the bordering woods, light on her feet. Jaali's legs, unused to movement for the past few weeks, were reluctant to follow, but he pressed on anyway. Going into the woods at night didn't seem like the wisest thing to do, but what other choice did he have?

The coat he had on, the only one he had been allowed to bring with him to prison, was not thick enough for the nocturnal chill, and soon his whole body shook convulsively, his teeth chattering, and his gloveless fingers tingling. "Ebba, how far are we going?" They had been running for over an hour with no evident destination in sight. "I don't want to sound ungrateful, but I may freeze soon."

Ebba stopped and looked at him, her eyes barely visible. She opened the bag she had been carrying and pulled a woolen wrap from it. "Use this. It's not much, but it'll help. We are less than an hour away, but we can't slow down now."

With the shawl around his shoulders, Jaali felt a little warmer. "Where are we going, Ebba?"

They resumed their track through the trees and the snow. Jaali had been afraid of the wild animals that roamed those woods at night, but they hadn't seen a single one. There was an eerie stillness to the night—no breeze, no animal noises. It was almost as if nature itself had stopped to let them go through.

"Years ago, I was in a bad place." The woman slowed down just enough to let him catch up to her. His legs, no longer used to snow, made it hard to navigate through its thickness. "Nobody in town would even talk to me. My own family shunned me and then moved to another village far away, not wanting to be associated with the devil's mark. I was lonely and hurting."

The painful familiarity of her story made his heart ache. "What did you do?"

"I ran away—one day I just started walking hoping to never come back." Her voice quivered. "I think I hoped some animal in the woods would find me more attractive than my own people. I wanted to die, but instead, I found this place."

His years in indenture had taught him one thing: death was not the worst thing that could happen to someone. In fact, at times he had sought the solace and peace of death. Anything would have been better than the life of pain, humiliation, and desperation he had been kidnapped into.

"I kind of stumbled upon it. Literally." She giggled, the sound so foreign coming from her, Jaali didn't realize what it was at first. "There it was, my shelter, my own little haven of peace. I kept it a secret all these years. Not that any of them would even think of following me into the woods." Bitterness came back to her voice. "It's a good place to hide until we can figure out what to do."

Jaali fell behind her, his step becoming more labored. The weeks of captivity were rearing their ugly heads—

living in semidarkness and having a minuscule space to move about had obviously affected his level of energy. The mere thought of walking another yard weighed heavily on him.

"Ebba, I need to rest. I'm not feeling very good." Ebba threw him an over-the-shoulder glance, but continued walking.

"Won't be long now, Jaali. Think of your wife and gather the courage to keep going."

Her simple words hit a chord. The image of Milenda as he had last seen her a couple of days ago appeared vivid as day in front of him. He couldn't reach out to her, but he could almost feel her heat. A smile stretched across his lips, and his legs, suddenly lighter, sped up the pace. He would make it for her. Milenda was all that mattered, and he would crawl through the fires of hell if necessary to keep her safe.

The rest of their trek throughout the dark forest seemed to go a lot faster, his mind distracted by images and memories of his wife. He was so immersed in his own thoughts, he almost crashed into Ebba's back when she suddenly stopped.

"We're here," she announced in a whisper, as if afraid to bust the happy bubble.

Here looked like a big bundle of nothing. As Jaali strained his eyes, scanning the ground, he couldn't see anything that looked remotely like a shelter. "I don't see it."

The young woman turned around, her eyes accusing. "That's because you're not looking at it right."

Confused but unwilling to admit it, Jaali squinted and blinked but still couldn't see anything other than the trees and the brush.

Ebba sighed. "I'll show you." She took a few steps forward and began moving a thick wall of branches and leaves. For a second, Jaali thought she had lost her mind. Was she trying to go through the thick layer of brush? His eyes widened when she uncovered an empty space beyond it. "Let's go."

Was she telling him to go into that dark hole in the forest wall? "Isn't it dangerous?" Images of hungry wolves and other predators popped into his mind. In Natale, it was never a good idea to crawl into dark holes in the jungle.

"It's perfectly safe. I come here all the time." The thought that Ebba might be double-crossing him and bringing him into some kind of trap crossed his mind. He hesitated. She sighed again. "All right. I'll go first. Didn't take you for a coward." The jab stung. *Better a coward than dead.*

The tiny woman ducked and entered the darkness ahead, vanishing into it moments later. Jaali hurried to follow her. At first, he couldn't see anything, the door of greenery closing behind him. But gradually his eyes adapted to the darkness and he could see some luminescence coming from the walls of what turned out to be a tunnel of sorts.

"What's that glow?" Ebba was in front of him, so small she could walk almost upright.

"Bioluminescence," she replied, as if she expected anyone to know what that was. He searched in his brain inventory of trivia he had learned throughout his lonely years at the university but, even though the word sounded vaguely familiar, he couldn't make a connection. "Organisms that create their own light. In this case, a kind of ivy and some insects."

Unable to find anything even mildly interesting to say about it, Jaali contented himself with a whispered "wow" and continued to follow Ebba down the long tunnel. After a while, the ceiling stretched higher and he was able to stand upright. Later, the tunnel drained into an open space where the self-illuminated creatures glowed so brightly for a moment, Jaali thought they had reached the outdoors. Ebba had obviously been working on making that space as comfortable as possible. There were blankets and pillows thrown haphazardly on top of furry rugs, a flat rock she had turned into a table, some dishes, and a storage crate with mostly canned products.

"During the winter, the cave is warm because of the volcanic heat, and during the summer, it's cool since it's mostly underground and protected by the overgrowth of the forest." Ebba was peeling off her coats, and Jaali followed suit. It was rather warm in there. Almost as if they had suddenly walked into spring. "We will be safe here for now. Make yourself comfortable."

Ebba was wearing a pair of men's pants and a white linen shirt beneath all the layers of coats. She played with a gadget on the wall, and Jaali was surprised to see water pouring out of it and into the cup she was holding underneath it. A natural spring. This girl was crafty indeed.

"Here, drink some water. Pick a spot and rest." Ebba poured herself another cup, took a long drink, and then sat down by one of the walls, adjusting a couple of pillows behind her. "I'm going to take a long nap."

Jaali watched her from across the room. She had undressed her coats but not her scarf, which still covered most of her head and face.

"You don't need to hide from me, Ebba." His eyes were heavy with sleep, but he needed to tell her that, to make sure she understood he didn't think any less of her because of her birthmark.

The woman stayed still for a moment, then began unwrapping the scarf from around her head, slowly, almost fearfully.

"I know how it feels to be different," Jaali told her, his eyes beginning to stubbornly close despite all his best efforts to prevent it. "Don't hide who you really are, Ebba. Not from me. Not from Milenda."

Ebba's hair, now freed from the fabric that confined it, fell thickly over her shoulders. Jaali's consciousness was quickly dimming, but he smiled at the sight of her relaxed stance even as he surrendered to the demanding arms of slumber. There was another good reason to smile—he was one step closer to his wife.

SICKNESS

MILENDA

Something wet and cold prodded her, first on her arm and then on her face. She tried to focus her eyes, still heavy with sleep, and met two great big green eyes staring right at her. Milenda giggled. "Silly Mjusi, you gave me a fright."

The flying lizard nudged her again with a tiny growl. When that didn't work, he took a mouthful of blanket and pulled it away from her, the cold air of the morning making her shiver. Giving up on sleep, Milenda sat up slowly, willing her stomach to stay stable and agreeable. The last few days had been rough. Every movement, everything she ate or drank, caused her insides to turn inside out. She could almost hear Mama Nyeusi tsking her, "You have to eat, child. Nothing good ever came of starving oneself."

The fact was she did want to eat, but her body wouldn't hear of it. With no access to doctors or even her traditional herbs, Milenda was at a loss as to what to do. She did the only thing she knew how—drank a lot of water, rested as much as she could, and prayed to Yemanjá to make her better and fit again.

"All right, Mjusi, I'll get up." As slowly as a slug, the disheveled princess got onto her feet and followed the small dragon out. "Where's the fire, my friend?"

Mjusi led her away from the cave and closer to where the other wyverns were gathered. Impatient with her slowness, the *msitu* took a few steps forward and then circled back around her as if to say, "Hurry up, will you?" Milenda, lightheaded and nauseated, chuckled under her breath. Mjusi was turning out to be Mama Nyeusi's replacement, always prodding her into action, always fussing over her.

As they approached, Milenda noticed one of the little dragons slumped on the ground, Mama Msitu, tapping her head gently against it and whimpering.

"What's wrong with Kijani?" Not sure of their gender, she had named the two smaller ones after their colors: this one for green and the other Zambarau for purple.

Milenda attempted more speed but managed only to make herself dizzier. Slowing down, she took a few large but measured steps toward the creature and slowly knelt down by it. The small dragon had its eyes closed and yelped quietly while the mother dragon licked its head with her long biforked tongue.

"What hurts, little one?" Milenda scanned the body of the dragon, but couldn't see anything out of place. Even after her time living with the wyverns, she was still cautious about touching them for fear they may not appreciate it. Mjusi, though, seemed determined she would touch the creature, pushing his hard head against her arms. "All right, Mjusi. I'll do it." She bent down a little farther and touched the dragon timidly at first, testing the waters. "Does this hurt? What about this?"

She examined each hind leg but found no broken bones, but when she was about to examine the front legs, she noticed a small puddle of blood on one of its talons. After further examination, she saw a large piece of metal buried between two of its claws.

"Sweetie, I have to pull it out." Milenda was nervous. She had grown to love these beautiful creatures, but they were not Mjusi who had grown up with her, the closest thing to a sibling she had ever had. There was no telling what the little one would do when she tried to pull that out. It might snap and bite her. Yet she couldn't let it suffer like that either. "I'll be as gentle as I can, all right?"

Kijani opened its eyes momentarily and made a little sound that Milenda took for a yes. She held on to his talon and, as gently as she possibly could, pinned the intruding metal between two fingers. At first, she tried to jiggle it a little, but it didn't budge. Taking a deep breath, she braced herself to pull on it hard. Mjusi had placed his head against her side, as if to comfort and encourage her. She took another breath and pulled.

The little dragon yelped as the big chunk of metal came loose from his claw, a spray of blood ejecting into the air. "It's out," Milenda said, relief immediately replaced with worry. There was a lot of blood coming out of the deep wound. "Mjusi, go fetch ice. Quickly."

Without delay, the *msitu* shuffled to the nearest pile of ice and dug into it with his powerful muzzle. When he came back to her shortly after, he was holding a big chunk of ice between his teeth. The princess smiled at him and applied the ice to Kijani's talon.

With one of her scarves, she improvised a bandage to hold it in place and then sat down to admire her handy work. *Not bad for a princess.* She had learned so much during the Trials and having to rescue Jaali in so many different occasions and ways. What was that thing Mama Nyeusi used to tell her? *Nothing you learn is ever useless.* Milenda smiled at the memory of her *yelorixá's* words. Gods, she missed her. For someone who had come into her life so late, the old woman sure had left a deep mark.

She watched as Mama Msitu spoiled the little one with attention while the other one played around its father. Mjusi had sat back down by her, his heavy skull on top of her outstretched legs, and his doleful eyes staring adoringly at her. "I love you too, my friend."

The sun was unusually warm for the season, so she stayed there, leaning on her arms, her face turned upward to the skies. Where was Jaali? She hadn't seen him in a few days. Even though she could sense him, he always seemed just out of reach, as if he was trying to hide from her. Which was not true, she was certain of it. Her trust in her husband was complete, unquestionable, and stood firm even through these few days of silence.

Freya had promised she would do something about this ridiculous idea of marrying him off to someone else, but a little part of her—especially when she was not fighting nausea—wondered what had happened. Was he married to someone else now? Not that it mattered. Such a marriage wouldn't be valid when they were still married to each other. But what if they had married him to someone else? Would Jaali accept it? Would he make love to this new wife like he did to her?

"No, no, no!" She shook her head so hard, the world wavered in front of her eyes. She held still, willing the dizziness to go away. "How can you be so stupid? Jaali would never betray you." Mjusi lifted his head and looked at her, tilting his neck. "I know, my friend. I'm going crazy. Now I even talk to myself."

"That's normally the first sign of impending madness." Why did Freya insist on sneaking up like that? It always gave her a fright. "Feeling lonely, are you?" The demigoddess circled around her until she was standing in front of her, gorgeous and scarcely clad. "I would too. You must miss your sweet man's loving."

Freya could be so inappropriate. But she did miss Jaali's loving—and his company, his voice, the way he looked at her as if she was a goddess herself. Where was he? What was he doing?

"Well, funny you should ask." The goddess's penchant to read her thoughts was extremely irritating. "As I was getting ready to pounce on those idiot children of mine, one of them—and truly the last one I'd expect to do something like this—stepped forward and saved your man's lovely bottom."

Milenda straightened up, hoping the small movement wouldn't cause any more dizziness. "How? How did she save him?"

"The sneaky little woman helped him escape during the night and took him to her hiding spot in the woods." Freya seemed truly awed by what she was telling Milenda, her eyes fixed somewhere far and a hand cradling her perfectly round chin.

"Why does she have a hiding place? Is she a thief of some kind?" Nothing was making much sense to her.

The goddess's eyes came back into focus on Milenda's. "She's an outcast. She was born with the devil's mark on her face. They treat her like she has the plague."

"Devil's mark? Is that dangerous?"

"It's a birth defect. A simple discoloration of the skin. It's neither dangerous or contagious. But the villagers are great believers in omens, and they see it as the mark of something evil. They won't even look at her straight." Was that a touch of anger Milenda could hear in Freya's voice? "If I were her, I would have murdered all of them in their beds by now." Milenda was very glad she wasn't.

"Who's this girl?" Milenda asked, a twinge in her chest telling her she already knew the answer.

Freya's beautifully proportioned face opened into a grin. "Your rival. The one who was to marry him."

Jaali was all alone in some hiding place in the forest with a woman who was to marry him. Her chest hurt, the weight of anxiety pressing down on her mercilessly. "Is she to be trusted?"

"Not to put her hands all over your lover?" Laughter burst out in small isolated explosions from the goddess's throat. "I can't promise you that. I probably couldn't be trusted, and she's been alone a very long time."

Nausea erupted with a vengeance, bile climbing her throat with the heat and destructive power of lava. Milenda gagged, bending over herself.

"By Thor's hammer! You are not doing well, Princess." The formerly teasing—even mocking—voice was replaced by what sounded an awful lot like worry. "Relax. The girl is as interested in your husband as he is in her. She had no intention of marrying your husband and doing the villagers' bidding. They've shunned her from birth. Why would she help them?"

Milenda tasted the vile acid on her tongue and gagged again. She wanted to be strong and energetic, to be ready whenever she needed to step in and help Jaali, but instead this illness had taken over. Tired all the time, she spent most of the day sleeping and the rest trying not to move for fear of vomiting. She was not used to being sick, and she was not enjoying it a bit.

"I will check on your man if you promise me to stay put and rest. You're a bit green." Freya stared at her, squinting her eyes. "Don't try to reach out to him. He is trying not to spook the woman."

The princess stretched herself on the ground, Mjusi scooting aside to give her some more room. "Tell him I love him."

"I think he knows that."

The goddess's flippant voice annoyed her. "Humans need to hear it even when they know it already." Her throat burned, and the churning in her abdomen told her this bout of nausea was far from over. "And don't tell him I'm sick. I don't want him to worry about me."

Freya rolled her eyes and waved a hand above her head. "Mortals! Who can ever understand them?"

"Promise me." Milenda's voice was hoarse, and her chest hurt from all the heaving. Her whole being longed for sleep.

"All right. I promise," Freya conceded with another eye roll. "You sleep. I'll take care of the rest."

With the goddess gone, Milenda was able to relax a little. She looked at the cave opening, but decided she would just stay put. The sun was still warm, and it would be light for another couple of hours at least. She could sleep right there. As if reading her mind, Mjusi came and curled beside her, his warm, scaly body acting as a shield against the lingering fingers of winter. She sighed and patted him. "Thank you, my friend. I can always count on you."

Tears rolled down her face as she faded into sleep. Despite the goddess's words and her own mind and heart telling her otherwise, Milenda couldn't help the tiny fear that was beginning to grow inside of her—fear of losing Jaali after all they had gone through together.

* * *

JAALI

With a swat at the annoying tickle on his face, Jaali flopped on his stomach still mostly asleep. The buzzing and tickling continued until he was wide awake. "Damn bug." He turned around, determined to smack the irritating creature, and found himself face-to-face with Freya.

"What are you doing here?" Shocked into total awareness, Jaali sat up quickly.

The goddess was half laying down beside him, holding the feather that had wakened him. Freya's proximity and familiarity still made him uncomfortable. He was not as freed of his demons as he thought he was after all. With Milenda they had all ran into hiding, but as soon as he was confronted with the sexual attention of others, they came back with a vengeance.

"You're no fun." She pouted like a little girl. Even though she had proved herself to be a great ally in spite of all their misgivings, Freya often showed the more inhuman side of her—unaware or uncaring about their human frailties and past traumas. "Your wife wouldn't care if we *played* a little."

Jaali pushed the covers aside and sprang to his feet. "I would care, Freya. No disrespect, but I am married to my wife body and soul."

Freya threw the feather away with gusto and groaned. "You know I could have you if I really wanted to, right?" He shivered, the familiar uncomfortable feeling of helplessness taking over. "Don't worry, I won't. Not because I see anything wrong with it, but Yemanjá would have my scalp if I did." She sat up, her arms crossed in front of her. "*Don't you touch a hair on his body, do you hear?*" Her impression of the Afrikan demigoddess was uncanny, and Jaali fought the urge to laugh.

Remembering Ebba, he looked urgently at her sleeping corner. She was still sleeping, curled under the blankets like a child, and for a fleeting moment, he worried. Was he going crazy and imagining Freya? Milenda's words from a while ago wafted to his ears, telling him that the gods were seen and heard only by those they chose. He relaxed.

"The gods don't like being seen." Freya's voice echoed through the tunnel. "That's why we normally appear in dreams instead. We prefer to stay in the background, mysterious and feared. However, after much deliberation, we've decided it's time our idiot villagers have a visual of their goddess."

He staggered, not sure of what she meant by that. "You're not going to hurt them, are you?" Bending down, Jaali picked up the blankets and began folding them to keep his jittery hands busy.

"As much as I would like to make them pay for their stupidity and disobedience, I won't hurt them." The goddess adjusted the ethereal white skirt she had wrapped loosely around her hips, one of her long and perfectly shaped legs peeking through the waist-high slit. "No, I will just make sure they know better than to cross me again."

"And Milenda and me?" He was almost afraid of asking, still not completely sure the goddess was fully on their side.

"You, sickening lovebirds, will soon be reunited." Frey laughed, a hand on her hips. "Not that being apart ever stopped you two from…." She made a vulgar gesture with her hands and exploded in laughter when Jaali blushed, his pale skin burning as if on fire.

To hide his embarrassment, Jaali dug through the box that held most of their food, a collection of tins and bags of dried foods. "I miss my wife." He hadn't meant to say it out loud, but the words escaped his lips nevertheless.

"She's not doing too well." This new information was dropped so casually, Jaali thought he had imagined it at first. Freya stared at him and shrugged. "Forgot to tell you. She's been unwell. Retching up a storm."

Anger boiled inside him. He was running out of patience with Freya's lack of empathy. "Why didn't you tell me? She needs help." It was not a question.

"The wyverns are taking good care of her. And I have been helping her too." Freya scowled, as if offended by his reaction. "She will be fine with rest and water."

He had stopped listening. His mind was already reaching out to Milenda on top of the mountain. At first, he didn't feel much, but soon nausea took over him as his mind stretched its fingers to her consciousness. She was sick, on the verge of vomiting, and as the queasiness left him, his physical body solidified beside her. Milenda was lying down inside the cave, in the fetal position, a container full of water next to her on the ground.

"*Msichana*, I'm here." He knelt beside her motionless body and swept his hand gently over her cheek. She stirred then, a deliberately slow movement to turn around and face him. His wife didn't look sick even though her lip curled and wrinkled in obvious discomfort. In spite of his worry, he had to smile at how she still surprised him with her beauty. Jaali fell in love again every time he looked at Milenda. "I'm here, love."

The Jewel sat up, her arms automatically folding around his neck and pulling him closer to her. "*Wimbo wa moyo*, where have you been? I missed you."

It had only been a few days since they were together, so her tears came as a shock. "Why do you cry? I'm all right. I'm here, *msichana*." He cupped his hand behind her head and kissed her cheek. "Didn't Freya tell you? I thought she told you—"

Milenda's sobs echoed close to his ears, her heart beating wild against his chest. "She did. I just worried."

Pulling her away from him, Jaali locked eyes with hers, red and wet with tears. "Worried about what? I was safe."

She sniffed, the sobs subsiding. Jaali wiped the tears from her cheeks with the back of his hand.

"You were alone with a woman of your own people, a way out of this mess I got us into. I thought… I thought you may consider marrying her." When he bristled, she rushed to add, "I wouldn't blame you. You deserve to be happy and in peace."

"Is that what you really think of me? That I would just abandon you because our marriage is inconvenient?" Jaali's heart was racing, his whole skin tightening in disappointment and anger. Was it possible that his wife, like everyone else in his life, thought so little of him? "How can you think that after everything we went through together? I love you, and

I don't care what kind of trouble that may bring us as long as we stick together."

Milenda's intense green eyes opened wide, and her hands clasped Jaali's head on both sides. "No, it's not like that. I just…." She burst out crying again, collapsing against his chest. "I don't know what's wrong with me lately. Everything upsets me. *Nasikitika*, Jaali, I'm so sorry."

His heart slowing down and his anger vanishing, Jaali tightened his hold around his wife, leaning his head against the top of hers. "I know you've been sick. Freya just told me. What's wrong?"

"I don't know. It's like the time I had a bout of malaria, only no fever or headache, just nausea and fatigue." She lifted her head to look at him. "So tired, Jaali. All I want to do is sleep."

Jaali felt her forehead, but she felt cool to his touch. Like she said, no fever. "Have you eaten?"

The Jewel shook her head. "Can't keep anything down. I wish I had Mama Nyeusi here. She'd know just what herbs to take."

Images of Ebba as she removed the contents of her bag danced in front of his eyes. She had lots of small containers and tiny bags that had piqued his curiosity. "Herbs and spices. When you're by yourself a lot, you need to know how to take care of health problems," she had explained as she placed the rainbow-colored vials on a makeshift shelf by one of the walls.

"Ebba can help." Milenda looked at him, her eyebrows raised into an arch. "Ebba Bjorgsson, the woman who was supposed to marry me." His jewel tensed up in his arms. "She's the one who helped me escape. She has a whole collection of herbs. I can ask her."

"Won't she be spooked by the fact that you can visit me from a distance, just like the other villagers?" Milenda wiggled against him, her eyes never leaving his.

"Maybe, but she doesn't seem to be superstitious like the others. I'll go there now." Jaali closed his eyes—he still needed to shut out all the outside stimuli to reach in and out—but his wife held on to him tightly as if afraid to lose him. "*Msichana*, it's all right. I think we can trust her."

Reluctantly, Milenda loosened her hold on him, and he closed his eyes again, reaching back to where he had left his shell. He knew right away he was back because the air was colder and there was an odor of moisture in the air from all the greenery that, stubbornly defying winter, grew inside the tunnels.

Eyes open and adjusting to the dim glow of the luminescent plants, Jaali searched for Ebba's sleeping form. She hadn't moved an inch since he left. Quietly, he approached and touched her shoulder, shaking her gently so as not to startle her. "Ebba, wake up."

The woman stirred and moaned a little as if annoyed to have her sleep cut short, but soon she was wide awake, sitting up against the wall and looking at him as if he had grown an extra head. "What's going on? Why aren't you asleep?"

Jaali was not sure how to approach the subject without sounding crazy or possibly possessed, which most of the villagers already believed he was. "My wife is sick, and she needs your help."

Ebba rubbed her eyes frantically. "Wait, am I dreaming? Did you say what I just heard?" Jaali nodded, and he watched as her face went through a gamut of different expressions—disbelief, fear, and then wonder. "How can you possibly know that?"

The truth was multifaceted. Which part was the least harmful? Telling her he was in direct contact with Freya, their revered and feared huntress goddess or that he could teleport himself to wherever Milenda was?

"Don't be scared, please. The villagers think my wife is a witch, but she was given this gift by an Afrikan goddess. It's not magic; it's a trait she inherited from her ancestors." Ebba's eyes looked ready to burst off their sockets. "She can either come to me or she can let me come to her, no matter how far we are from each other. She saved my life because of this gift of hers."

He scanned Ebba's face, trying to decipher her current expression. Her eyes were still round like apples, and her mouth was stretched into a tight, thin line. For a moment, he was not even sure she was breathing. "Ebba? Are you all right?"

"You could bring her here? Right now?" She licked her lips and wiped her face with her hand.

"Yes, and maybe you could help her with some tea or—she's sick, Ebba. I don't know what to do." Jaali was past cautious, past scared. He was in a panic, urgently wanting to help his ailing wife at any cost. "If I bring her here, will you promise not to judge her and help her? She's harmless."

Silence enveloped them. Jaali wanted to rush her, but he knew it would be better to allow her the time to get to a decision on her own terms. It was hard though to stand there watching her face go through the emotions while she paced around the soft floor of the tunnel room. He interlaced his fingers behind his back to prevent himself from grabbing and shaking her into a decision.

When she finally stopped and looked up at him again, he could have sworn hours had passed. "Well? Will you do it?"

Ebba's face, now freed from the cover of the scarf, lit up in a smile. "I can't wait to see it. Yes, I will help you however I can."

Jaali fought the urge to draw the small woman into a hug and offered her a big smile instead. "Thank you. Can't wait for you to meet her. I'll call her now." From the corner of his eye, Jaali saw Ebba reach for her scarf. "And don't cover yourself. Milenda is not one to judge."

It took only seconds for the Jewel to appear next to him, still laying down, knees bent almost to her chest. Jaali sat beside her and pulled her into his arms. "*Msichana*, meet Ebba."

Ebba took a few steps in their direction, her eyes glowing in wonder. "How did that happen?"

Milenda looked up at the other woman and smiled. "Nice to meet you, Ebba. We don't know how it happens. It just does." The Fjorden woman placed a hand on her face, in an attempt to cover her mark. "Thank you for helping my husband. I hate that I couldn't do anything other than hide."

Jaali chuckled. "I always seem to be in need of help from a female." Milenda's laughter soon turned into a string of retching noises. "Can you help her? She says she's always nauseated and tired."

Ebba scuffled to her herb collection and spent the next few minutes looking through them and then warming up some water for tea. When she came back to them, she had a mug of steaming, sweet-scented brew between her hands. "Here, sip on this. Be careful. It's hot. It'll help with the nausea."

Jaali propped Milenda against him while she took small sips from the cup the other woman had given her. "Tastes fresh and sweet." She drank some more and relaxed against her husband. "It's good."

Forgetting to hide her birthmark, Ebba sat back on the floor, facing the couple. "Peppermint leaves. Tasty and relaxes the muscles of your stomach so it soothes the feeling of nausea." Jaali smiled at her, relieved that Milenda seemed in less discomfort. "Can I ask you a personal question, Milenda?"

Milenda nodded as she brought the cup up to her lips one more time. Jaali bent down lightly and kissed her cheek close to her ear.

"When did you have your last bleeding?"

The question stunned Jaali but didn't seem to bother his wife who just continued to sip on her tea, a hand now resting loosely on his leg. "What do you mean? She hasn't been hurt—"

Milenda giggled. "She means the monthly bleeds, *wimbo*

wa moyo. I don't know. It's been a while."

Jaali's heart began a furious race in his chest. He remembered it well. They had been on the ship still. "You haven't had one since you've been with the wyverns?"

Milenda thought about it, but when she suddenly stiffened against him, he knew: he was going to be a father.

THE SURPRISE

Milenda

Mjusi hadn't left her side since she came back from her visit to Jaali's hiding place. You'd think he knew. If he did, he was a lot sharper than she was. Not once had she thought her malaise was because of pregnancy. Her naivete about life in general was playing tricks on her. Mama Nyeusi would have known. She would have seen and identified the signs right away. Milenda had no life experience to back her up. Growing up within the walls of the royal palace surrounded by servants and with no mother to rely on for common female wisdom, she was blissfully ignorant of so many things.

A hand flat on her belly and the other cradling a mug of Ebba's deliciously soothing tea, the princess wondered about her condition. She was with child. Not once in her life and ever since being married had she ever considered the possibility. Which was stupid in itself. After all, Jaali had been accepted as a Contender in the Trials for her hand in marriage because he had been found fertile. Not many males in Natale were able to produce children anymore. Centuries of inbreeding had begun to show unexpected and dire consequences. Then why hadn't she even considered the fact that she could be pregnant? She may be naive about a lot of things, but she knew how babies were made, and the gods knew neither she or Jaali had been trying to prevent pregnancy.

Milenda leaned against the wall and allowed herself to get lost in her own thoughts. She had a lot of questions that only she could answer. Was she happy about this baby? Was this pregnancy a good or bad thing in the long run? Was she going to be able to be there for her child? To see her—or him—grow into an amazing person. To grow into a royal heir....

"What have I done?" Mjusi lifted his head, startled by her voice. "I'm creating another innocent victim for the Elders. My child will be prosecuted and will have to live in hiding, like I do." She hung her head and tears rolled down her cheeks. Her poor child, born to a princess with a target on her forehead and an ex-slave hunted down by his own people. What kind of future would their child have?

In her head, she heard Mama Nyeusi's voice. "Don't be daft, child. Things will change. You and Jaali will change the way things are, and your baby will be happy and grow in peace. We're all counting on you."

That was the problem. There were too many people— including a couple gods—expecting her to perform some kind of miracle and change the way things were in Natale.

To somehow break the Elders' control over her nation, erase all oppression, and bring the kind of peace and justice her people deserved. She was just a young woman, small and not too knowledgeable of the ways of the world. What did she know about leading a nation in a revolution? What resources would she use when most of the military and political bodies of her nation were well tucked in the Council of Elders' pocket?

It was ludicrous to think she could have any control or influence over a whole nation blinded by and dependent on old beliefs and traditions. A country of people so fearful of the wrath of the gods and so trusting in the wisdom of those in power, they were paralyzed to act on their own behalf.

"I'm not the right woman for the job, Mjusi." She sat the mug on the floor next to her and wiped the tracks of tears with the back of her hand. "I don't know what Yemanjá is thinking, trusting me to be brave enough to do the right thing."

The nausea had subsided thanks to the tea, but now her chest was filled with butterflies of anxiety, fluttering their wings so fast it was hard to breathe. Milenda wrapped the *nguba* around her shoulders and emerged from the cave into the chilly night. The black velvet of the sky was studded with diamond-like stars that winked at her mischievously, like children in a silly game of truth or dare.

"Don't ask me any questions." Milenda lifted her eyes to the skies above, wondering if the stars were the blinking eyes of the gods, watching over the earth and playing with their mortal children, mere puppets in a universe-size dollhouse.

"I don't have any answers."

The wyverns were asleep, a giant mound of flesh and scales in a corner of the mountain shelf, all curled against each other. *That's what a family should be like.* Always together, joined by love and sustained by mutual trust and respect. Not like her own or Jaali's, divided by fears, distrust, and prejudice. At least her father had come around to be a real father to her however belatedly, and she could only hope that if or when they went back he would still be there for her. *She'll need an ally in power.* She also still hoped against all odds that Jaali's father, whenever he came back, would choose to stick to his son's side instead of the villagers'.

Milenda reached out to Jaali. Gently, not wanting to wake him up. He had such a stunned look on his face when she left him earlier that day. How did he feel about the baby? Was he as scared as she was?

She saw his dear face, relaxed into peaceful sleep, his long hair spread around it like a halo. Her heart fluttered as it always did when she looked at her northern man. Jaali was lovely, his skin and hair the color of moon beams, tall and covered in lean muscle built on hard work and heartache.

I love you so much. She didn't dare say it out loud and wake him up. With a feathering of fingers, she pulled a lock of his hair from his forehead and tucked it behind his ear. She touched her lips to his cheek. She was carrying this man's baby inside of her, the child of the man she loved more than life itself and who made her stronger than she ever thought possible. Her lips still tingling from the contact with his skin expanded into a smile that quickly climbed to her tear-rimmed eyes. She was having Jaali's baby, a little bit of him and her. It wouldn't be an easy ride for any of them, but in her heart, the seed of happiness had taken root and grew already. *We're going to have a baby, wimbo wa moyo. The three of us against the world.*

***

JAALI

"Are you going to spend the whole day staring at that wall?" Ebba's voice snapped him from the semitrance he was in. Enough at least to make him move his glance away from the green wall and into the small woman across from him. "You really didn't know?"

Shock was too mild a word to describe what he'd felt when he found out he was going to be a father. He and Milenda had been so busy running for their lives, trying to stay one step ahead of their enemies, that he had never considered the possibility. Truth be told, having been an indent most of his life, he had never thought about becoming a father someday. Survival had always been the first and foremost priority in his life—at least until he met Milenda.

Everything had changed then. He still had survival as a constant companion and need, but it paled by comparison with the love he felt for his wife. His Jewel was now his savior, his way out of the hell he had been living in for years. His princess was the light at the end of the very long and winding tunnel of his youth.

And now a child, knitted from his and Milenda's genetic yarn. It sounded impossible, like a fairy tale off a childhood book, a miracle. How wondrous it was that a nobody like him could have created life inside someone as beautiful and special as the Jewel? Milenda's voice whispered in his head as it always did, telling him he wasn't a *nobody*. "You're everything, *wimbo wa moyo*, everything." Even in the obscurity of the tunnels, Jaali's face glowed, warmed by the sun of her remembered words.

The sound of a soft chuckle brought him back to the here and now. Ebba was staring at him, a crooked smile on her face. "The look on your face! Priceless." She threw a small pebble at him with a raucous laugh. "If that's what you look like when you're in love, I'm glad I'm marked by the devil."

Jaali threw the rock back at her, feigning outrage. "Well, you'd look like this too if you just found out you were going to be a father."

She laughed even louder, folding at the waist. "That's for sure. Considering I'm a woman, I'd be shocked right and proper."

Realizing what he had said, Jaali burst out in laughter too. In spite of the initial shock and wonder, there were bubbles of happiness growing inside of him, wanting to spill out. He kept them inside for fear that if he let them out, they would pop and burst. Eager to hold his wife and whisper his joy into her ear, Jaali was antsy, full of an energy that coursed through him, a wildfire getting harder and harder to contain.

"I'm just so happy—and so scared at the same time."

The fact that he trusted a stranger enough to open up to her like that took him by surprise. He was not used to that, but something about Ebba exuded an aura of trustfulness. She, like himself, had always been the odd duckling, the outcast treated according to what she looked like and not who she really was. In a way, opening up to her was inevitable. Yet, still unsettling.

"For what it's worth, I don't think your wife is a witch." Ebba had stopped laughing. "And the only spell she had you under is love."

Jaali squeezed his hands between his knees, beaming. "Thank you. And for what it's worth, I don't believe that's the devil's mark either."

An awkward silence fell between them, their eyes wondering away from each other's and hiding on the ground before them. Ebba fiddled with the cup she had in her hand for a moment. Then she stood up and directed her attention to the kettle boiling over the small fumerole. "What about some tea?"

Neither of them were obviously comfortable sharing their feelings, both having spent too much time by themselves, suspicious of all and everything. The tea provided the diversion they needed to settle back into the cozy, easy companionship they'd developed for the past few days.

That night Freya came to visit. This time Jaali was waiting, fully expecting her appearance. "You've heard then."

The goddess stood, half naked and gorgeous, her hands firmly on her hips. "Can't believe I didn't see it earlier."

She pinned her lower lip between her teeth, a look of confusion on her face. "How did that happen?"

Jaali laughed. "Do I have to explain how babies are made?" Freya threw him a dirty look, but he could tell she was amused, her lips half turned into a smile. "What do we do now? Do I join her in the mountains? I don't want her to be alone through this."

"She's not alone. The wyverns are good company, and they keep her fed and safe." Was she that out-of-touch with humans that she truly believed those creatures, no matter how friendly and amazing, could replace the company of a loved one? "But I do have a plan. Your father should be back in the village within the next couple weeks. The snow has melted enough that he will be heading home soon."

He could barely remember his father. A vague memory of a tall, silver-haired man with ocean-colored eyes that went misty every time they landed on his mother. Funny how he remembered that—the unmistakable glow of love in his father's eyes. "What if he sides with my sister?"

Freya waved her hand in the air. "Your sister is an idiot who doesn't have half a brain. She's more worried that her children will now have to share your father's patrimony with you." Jaali went still. "Your father is a respected man in these parts, a *borgmästare,* the leader of Örebro. He owns quite a bit of land and a couple houses, not to mention horses and other farm stock. He's a rich man, Jaali, and your sister just saw those riches getting thinner when you arrived in town alive and well."

No, he couldn't believe that his sister would be that

much of a mercenary and willing to ruin his life in order to inherit material goods. Then again, he really didn't know her anymore. Maja was irrationally angry at him for the misfortune that had fallen upon him and his family. She had been older than him by a few years at the time of his kidnapping, but he remembered her vaguely at best.

"Maja thinks that if it's established that you're not totally well in the head and, even better, if you marry someone like Ebba, your father will have no choice but to keep you off his will. More for her and her children." The goddess paced in front of him, frowning. "Well, I guess maybe she's not that dumb after all. Just extremely greedy."

Jaali slumped against the wall, shoulders drooping forward, his hair falling over his face. How stupid of him to think he would be received with open arms, welcomed into the bosom of his family. Whatever family he had all those years ago was not there anymore.

"Why so gloomy, young Fjorden? I have been betrayed by every single member of my family and yet, you don't see me moping around, do you?" Uncharacteristically, Freya sat down next to him, his body instantly flinching away from any contact. "Still don't trust me. I suppose I can't blame you for being squeamish around people after what you went through." Even though she seemed to be talking more to herself than him, Jaali threw her a nervous sideways glance. He was never sure of the goddess's real intentions.

"What's your plan? After my father comes back."

The goddess's pensive expression changed to the usual mix of sarcasm and cockiness. "Don't worry that pretty head of yours. Let Freya, the Great Warrior, work on it." Jaali didn't remember any mention of her as a warrior anywhere in the books he had read about northern mythology, but he thought it wiser not to mention it to her. "All I can say is that it will be truly spectacular."

She jumped to her feet in a feline-like move, shook some imaginary dust from her threadbare clothing, and threw her luscious hair over her shoulder. "I have to go. My idiot husband is off somewhere in *Jotunheim* fraternizing with the giants, and there is one of his beautiful warriors in need of my attention."

The voluptuous goddess licked her lips, leaving no doubt as to what she meant by attention. Without any goodbyes or warning, she vanished. Being the center of Freya's attention certainly promised as much pleasure as pain. Jaali mumbled a quiet prayer of thanks he wasn't the one garnering such notice, and sliding all the way to the ground, he fell asleep.

NORTHERN LIGHTS

When Kijani and Zambarau came back close behind the wyvern mother, Mjusi ran to greet them. The usual clicking of tongues and a plenitude of huffs and puffs ensued, bringing a smile to Milenda's face. Now that she understood the significance of such noises, she could anticipate the return of the creatures every morning. Mjusi rarely went with the rest of the family, choosing to stay with her instead, and she sometimes worried whether she was inadvertently keeping him from bonding with his new family.

Milenda looked up in the direction where every morning the four dragons took off flying, their impressive wings creating a maelstrom of air and snow. She wondered where they went and what was up there that made them take that daily trip. Unlike Tausi, who always brought dinner after his excursions later in the day, they never brought anything back, but always came back energized and happy.

"Maybe I'll go up there tomorrow." Mjusi tilted his head

like a bird and blinked his big green eyes at her. She giggled. "You heard me right. Do you want to come with me?"

Nausea had faded into almost nothing since she had begun drinking Ebba's tea a few days ago and had been replaced by a renewed zest for life she was finding hard to control. When her husband came to see her the night before, she had been a bundle of energy ready to explode.

"Jaali!" Her arms skimmed his shoulders and crossed behind his neck, bringing his mouth close to hers. "I missed you."

With a chuckle, Jaali wrapped his arms around her waist. "You saw me last night. What's going on?"

A current of electricity ran through her, lighting up her *matangazos* and making them burn hot and cold. She didn't answer. Pulling him even closer, she grazed her lips across his, pulling gently with her teeth until Jaali groaned in pleasure.

They had stumbled into the cave, entangled in each other's arms and legs, items of clothing dropped and forming a trail behind them. Jaali shivered in anticipation as his wife peeled every layer of clothing he had on until his bare skin tingled in the chilly air and under the touch of her hands.

"Is it safe?" His voice, thick with desire had echoed like a song in her ears. She giggled. It was a bit too late to think about safety. "I mean, with the baby."

Her heart soared. She loved that man. "Of course, it's safe. How else is she going to know how much her parents love her and each other?"

Jaali peppered kisses along her neck and shoulder where

her shirt had slid off and left naked. "So it's a girl, is it?" She giggled again, and he pulled on her shirt until her arms were freed and her breasts were bare. He cupped a hand over one of her breasts and moaned. "You're so beautiful."

Milenda shrugged the rest of her clothes off and flattened her hands to his chest, pushing him until Jaali's back was against the cold stone wall. She loved the whiteness of his skin stretched across the muscles on his hairless chest into his perfectly muscled biceps. A new wave of energy coursed through her, a river of feverish yearning that left her breathless. Slowly, she brushed her fingers along his skin, down from the Adam's apple, lingering over his chest for a moment, and then reaching down to his hard abs and lower still. They let out a moan at the same time, the warmth of her hand meeting and wrapping around the heat of his desire.

"I love you, *wimbo wa moyo*," she whispered, her lips hovering just above his. "I want you."

Jaali slid his hands down to her buttocks and pulled her off her feet, flipping places with her. Her back now against the wall, Milenda wrapped her legs around his waist and braced herself on his shoulders. She felt him throbbing against her, their heat mixing and mingling. Jaali, his hands burning against the back of her thighs, pulled her up slightly before burying himself inside her. It was still strange and wonderful to her how well they fit together, as if they had been made for each other—two sides of one whole.

Her husband's gasps of pleasure as she rhythmically rose and lowered herself on him made her smile and want even more. They floundered about until they were both on the ground, Milenda propped with her hands against his chest, rocking back and forth on top of him, her head thrust behind and *matangazos* blazing. They came together in a flood of intense sensual overload before collapsing on each other, gasping for air.

Milenda sighed, her body responding at the memory. Her whole being vibrated with the burst of nervous energy she seemed cursed to carry with her these past couple days. She needed to do something. Making love to her husband again was not an option. Her eyes wandered to the top of the mountain, and a new yearning lodged itself in her chest. She was going to climb up that side of the mountain and watch the winter skies before they gave way to spring. With her mind made up, she was able to focus on the daily lazy routine of eating, resting, and playing with the young *msitus*.

As soon as the light of day began to fade, Milenda began preparing for the long climb. Even though it wasn't very cold on the wyvern's ledge, she knew that Old Man Winter was still making sure creatures everywhere knew he was very much alive and reigning over these lands. She layered her Fjorden clothes, one on top of the other, until she resembled one of those Wazi icons carved of the bark of trees—short and rotund.

"Where in heaven's name are you going?" It was Jaali who had materialized silently behind her. "Isn't it a bit late to go out exploring?"

She waddled to her husband, restricted by the thick layer of the pants she was wearing. "I'm going to the summit to watch the night skies."

She had said this with such enthusiasm, Jaali laughed. "Because you can't see it from here? Where it's warm and safe."

Milenda tried to wrap him in a hug, but the bulk of her clothing would only allow a half of one. She giggled. "Damn clothes. I'm too…" She looked for words to describe that restlessness she had been feeling since the nausea abated. "I don't know. I have all this energy cooped up inside of me."

Jaali combed his hair with his fingers. "I noticed." Milenda's *matangazos* burned, the wave of heat spreading from her shoulder to her face. "So you're going to climb a mountain. You know, we could repeat what we did last night."

She laughed, half embarrassed by the memory of how uninhibited she had been the night before. "That would be nice, but—I know it's strange—but I have this yearning to go up there. I don't know why. It's like it's calling me."

"I'll go with you, but you can't go dressed like that. You can barely move."

Milenda stared down at herself. She looked a lot like an odd fur-lined sausage. Jaali was right. How was she going to climb over rocks and snow if she could barely move her arms? She frowned, her shoulders slumping forward, and her lips pressed into a thin line.

"The secret of staying warm while still being able to move is how you layer the clothes." Jaali's voice made her tilt her head and raise her eyebrows. "I'll explain."

For the next half hour, Jaali stripped off the thick coating of furs and linens and taught her how to layer more effectively. By the time he was finished, Milenda was overheated but able to move around a lot easier. Her husband was wearing inside clothes, and for a second, forgetting he couldn't really feel the temperature while projecting, she worried about him.

They began their climb under the curious stares of the wyverns, all settled for the night. Mjusi followed them, flapping his wings and switching back and forth from flying to walking beside them, clucking like a mother hen. The climb was steep, but the rocks that butted out from the sides of the mountain created an easy enough staircase to navigate. Milenda couldn't say how long it took to get to the top, distracted and pleased as she was to have her husband next to her. It'd been a while since they had done something together other than lay side by side in that cave, making love.

When Jaali abruptly stopped in front of her and offered his hand to pull her up to a flat shelf, she was shocked to find they had arrived at the top. Mjusi shook his head up and down in long fluid moves and flapped his wings in excitement. Was it possible the *msitu* was also happy to be doing something together with both of them?

"We're here, *msichana*," Jaali announced unnecessarily.

They were on a small shelf on the rock, surrounded by short, hardy shrubs that had somehow managed to stay green throughout the fierce winter. The princess stared behind her, in the direction from where they had come, and gasped in awe. The velvety dark mantel of the night, jewel-studded and infinite, spread in front of and above them. On the bottom, and stretching as far as the eye could see, lay the darkness of the forest and the promise of the whiteness of the valley beyond.

"This is beautiful," Milenda whispered, afraid of breaking the spell. The view from the top was magical. She had never seen anything like it.

"Wait until you see the northern lights," Jaali whispered back, leaning against her back and wrapping his arms around her. She recalled him saying those exact same words shortly after they had arrived in *Isvärld.* "Shall we sit?"

They sat on that flat rock, Milenda leaning back on her husband, his legs bookending her thighs. Jaali opened the small bag he had packed and produced their *nguba,* the northern design almost glowing in the twilight as he unfolded it over the two of them. Silence surrounded them and lulled them into the sense of peace they had been craving. Mjusi had stopped pacing around and dropped by his human friends, curled upon himself and fell asleep.

"Mama Nyeusi is going to be so happy when she finds out about the baby." Milenda spoke in whispers. "Do you think Yemanjá knows now?"

Jaali dropped a kiss by her ear. "Who knows? I don't understand these gods and goddesses. At all."

At that time, an extraordinary thing happened. The sky, dark until that moment, lit up with fireworks—at least, that's what Milenda thought at first. Showers of white, blue, and lavender ribboned the dark blue sky as if the canvas of an artist. The forest below was suddenly alive with reflections and shadows that moved and sparkled, bringing the trees to life. The whiteness, just out of reach, turned a light shade of ocean blue. The gods had brushed and saturated the night skies with rainbows of oil paints.

"Now, that's what I call magic." Jaali tightened his hold on her, nestling his face against hers. He was warm and cold at the same time, smelling of pine trees and snow. She turned her face just enough to capture his lips in a long kiss.

"No," she whispered over his mouth, the *nguba* all the way up to her neck and the heavens still strutting their feathers around them. "You, here with me, that's the real magic."

THE RETURN

Jaali

"Let's go."

Jaali stared up at Freya's impressive body, surprised by her sudden appearance and even more so by her command. "Go where?"

"Back to the village. Your father is back." The demigoddess tapped her foot and crossed her arms, her lower lip caught between her teeth. "There's no time to waste, boy. Let's go."

Jaali jumped to his feet, mumbling under his breath and tempted to point out to Freya that they were at least a day's walk from town. Ebba had stepped out a few minutes before the goddess made her dramatic appearance.

"I have to wait for Ebba. Not leaving without her." Not that he could find his way back without her anyway, but he owed her big, and he fully intended to pay her back.

"Oh, you're bringing the girl with you?" Freya frowned as if she smelled something unpleasant.

Jaali rolled his eyes, folding his blankets and tidying up the sleeping space as he did every morning. "Well, she did save me from an unwanted marriage."

"Exactly! I'll never understand how she could back out of marrying such a delicious morsel as yourself." The goddess's words made Jaali's stomach turn. "The girl is dumb." She sighed. "But if you must, yes, bring her with you."

Trying to keep his empty stomach from emptying itself even further, Jaali sat by the wall, knees drawn up to his chin. "Are you sure this is the right thing to do?"

Freya threw her arms up in the air, her full breasts bouncing and threatening to escape from the hug of the threadbare bodice she was wearing. "What's with my children lately? What makes you believe you can doubt my judgment?"

"Sorry, Freya, but it makes me nervous to think of going back to where people want to kill my wife and marry me off to someone else."

The beautiful woman crouched beside him. "Just have faith in me for once." Strangely, her voice had taken on a timbre he had never heard before. She was serious. For once the goddess had abandoned her cockiness and know-it-all attitude in favor of genuine concern. "Trust me."

For the first time since Freya had appeared and interfered with his life, Jaali felt comfortable around her. He believed her intentions and suddenly trusted she would do right by him and Milenda.

"I'll be on my way as soon as Ebba is back. We should

be able to be back in town by night fall." His body relaxed. "What about Milenda?"

Freya got back on her feet, smoothing out invisible wrinkles in her sparse coverings. "First, you get yourself to Örebro. Then we'll worry about your little wife."

He was not going to argue. Not now that the goddess seemed to be in earnest about helping them. With the usual lack of closure, Freya vanished into thin air just as Ebba emerged through the tunnel.

"Did I hear voices?" She rubbed her arms and looked around, suspicious.

Jaali laughed. "Yes, you did."

It was not easy to explain he had been having a conversation with a demigoddess, but Ebba took it all in stride. Having lived outside normal social interaction seemed to have prepared her to accept things others would find difficult to understand. She listened to his account of the recent visit from Odin's wife with the same interest as if he'd have told her a story about a deer or a rabbit. Ebba's curiosity was perhaps a natural consequence of her isolation, but made her by far one of the best listeners he had ever met.

In no time, they had packed what they were bringing with them and stored everything else. They left the tunnel together, and Jaali looked back one last time and was surprised how well it was hidden. A whole day of walking through the heavy forested land awaited them. The snow had begun thinning out, but under the shade of the trees, it still held enough thickness to make for a difficult trek.

It was dark already when they emerged from the forest into the white valley. Exhausted and hungry, Jaali and his companion buckled their snowshoes to their boots and began the long walk across the subtle waves of snow that stood between them and the village. Faint twinkling lights in the distance reminded them it was indeed there and beckoned them forward.

"What do you think they're going to do when they see us?" The question had been nagging him ever since they'd left that morning. Jaali didn't want to be anxious, but he was. As much as he wanted to believe that his father would take his side and have enough influence over the villagers to change their minds, the truth was he had little hope. Events of recent memory didn't seem to support such an outcome.

Ebba had slowed down just enough to trudge through the snow, side by side with him. She was a faster walker than him, who was not used to these road conditions. She was also much lighter, which gave her an advantage when it came to deep snow. With his height and weight, it was all he could do not to sink all the way even with the snowshoes strapped on.

"They won't be happy with either of us." That went without saying. In his mind, he could see Maja's and Arvid's white faces turning purple with anger. "But, if the Lady is to be believed, maybe your father will manage to bring them to their senses. He's always been kind to me."

Jaali turned to look at her. Ever since they had first arrived at their hiding place, she had refrained from covering her face. Even then, with the cold wind buffeting their faces with the cruelty of a whip, she kept her face bare and visible. Proud.

"Really? My father has treated you well?" The hope that his father was not the superstitious and cruel type that had been plaguing Milenda's and his life ignited in his chest. "How's that?"

Still focused on the snow-covered road ahead, Ebba smiled. "Ever since your mother died, he's been a little withdrawn, but he has never treated me differently from the others and often invited me to his house for tea or a meal. I'm sure he was the target of much criticism by his advisers and family members, but he didn't heed any of their crap. He's a good man."

Jaali's heart soared, and in spite of his resolve not to have unrealistic expectations, a little seed of hope sprouted leaves as the town's buildings became more than shadowy dots in the horizon. Under the light of the moon and stars, they could now discern houses with their lit windows and white-mantled roofs. They would be in town in less than an hour.

The *gemenskap hus* stood in the center of the quaint little town frowning at them—or maybe warning them of what was inside. Jaali shook his head to dispel his fanciful thoughts and, after a quick glance at his companion, closed his fingers around the knocker. He knew it was all in his imagination, but he thought he heard the knocking sound reverberate through the air like the sounds of bells, loud and ominous. He admired Ebba's calmness, standing beside him, face uncovered and stoic composure when his insides were all turned upside down and twisted into knots.

The mechanical sound of the door unlocking punched Jaali's gut as effectively as a fist. Fighting a wave of nausea, he struggled to stand straight as the door slowly opened to let out a wave of heat and light. From within the house, the humming of voices quieted as the door opened wider to reveal the unexpected visitors. A sudden hush ran through the room until all they could hear was the crackling of the wood in the hearth.

Jaali stepped forward, his dry mouth making it difficult to swallow. "I'm here to see my father." For a moment, it was as if everyone was under a magic spell, paralyzed and silent. "Where's Vide Asker, my father?" he asked louder, his anger taking place of his fears.

The crowd that seemed to have gathered in the center of the room separated to allow a lone figure to come through. The man was as tall as Jaali, his face carved by early signs of life's many heartaches. "Who are you?"

Another step forward and Jaali's legs began shaking, weak from the long walk and the emotional shock of finally meeting his father. Images of a young self, covered in furs and jumping with excitement on a fishing trip with *Pappa,* invaded his thoughts. His eyes burned with unshed tears, and he braced himself on Ebba's shoulder.

"*Far*, it's me, Jaali, your son." He was not sure he had said it out loud. The word *far*, father, felt foreign in his tongue but pregnant with hope.

His father stopped shy of touching Jaali, his eyes latching on to his son's equally transparent eyes. "Jaali, *liten älg*, is that really you?"

The sound of his father's old nickname for him dissolved all his armor. His father had often addressed him as his little elk, Jaali's legs seeming to grow faster than the rest of his body as a child. Hearing the term of endearment was more than he could take. The tears that had been hovering in his eyes spilled over, rolling down his cheeks like rivulets of pain, longing, and love. The man he had always pictured in his memory as his father was real, not a construction of his imagination.

"*Pappa*...." The whole world blurred around the imposing figure of his father, and oblivious to all else, Jaali threw himself into the arms of the man who had given him life. Strong arms came around his shoulders and held him tight, hard muscle against hard muscle. For the first time since his arrival in *Isvärld,* he felt at home.

"Call the *Seiðmenn*," a voice yelled out and soon was followed by a crescendo of grumbling voices. "He must marry my brother right now."

Jaali, his face still wet with tears, raised his eyes to his sister. Maja was standing a few steps away from them, red in the face and waving her hands in the air as she ordered this man and the other to fetch the *seidr* practitioner.

An anger, so fierce it threatened to choke him, exploded in his chest. "I will not marry Ebba or anybody else. I'm already married."

The words screamed out with passion stopped everything and everyone in their tracks. Jaali's father, blond eyebrows knitted together, looked at Maja first and then at his son.

"What's this all about?" He stared at Maja again, who stuffed her hands in her apron's pockets, looking like a chastised child. "Why are you trying to marry your brother to Ebba?" Maja lowered her gaze to the floor. The older man's probing eyes turned to Jaali then. "And what do you mean you're married already?"

After much discussion and turmoil, Ebba, Jaali, and his father were allowed to sit quietly in a corner to relate everything that had happened in the past weeks. Maja tried to join the conversation more than once, but was quickly dismissed by her father. "I will talk to you after, Maja."

Jaali watched his father with interest and a lot of anxiety while they talked. His heart sped up when his father's eyes opened in shock at the news of whom he had married and then slowed as the older man's face relaxed into a smile at hearing his son talk about how much he loved Milenda. For his and Ebba's ears only, Jaali revealed his wife's true identity and didn't mince words to express how disappointed and hurt he was in his own sister's lack of compassion. By the time he was finished with the whole story, Vide Asker had paled, his lips curled down and eyes moist with tears. Still silent, he placed a comforting hand on Jaali's shoulder, and a sad smile replaced his frown.

When he stood up, the room went quiet, every eye falling on him. Jaali could tell he was a figure of some authority and respect among the villagers. Jaali watched with a sudden surge of love in his heart as his father took a few steps forward to place himself in the middle of the crowd and raised a hand to quiet the room even further.

"People of Örebro, hear me now." The ceremonial words were all telling. His father was going to make an announcement. "I understand how you were scared by recent events involving my son, Jaali, and his wife from a faraway land." The small crowd mumbled, and Vide stopped them with an open hand. "Just like in *Isvärld*, there are people in Afrika who are bad, but there are also those who are good and wish nothing else but to live their lives in peace and harmony with others." There was further mumbling, but no one dared arguing. "My daughter-in-law, Milenda, is one of the latter. She is one who will fight with all her might to end this abomination called indenture."

Jaali couldn't help but smile. His father remembered his wife's name. He was on their side, and gods willing their nightmare was almost over.

"She is not one of the *duivels* that prey on our children, neither is she a witch. The great Lady Freya has favored her, so why would you, mere mortals that you are, defy her judgment? Has she not come to you in a dream? Has she not warned you that if you insist on this injustice, doom will come upon all of you? Haven't you been visited by the great dragons? Have you grown so soft in the head you cannot understand all the signals?"

The grumbling had subsided. Jaali couldn't be sure whether his father's words had the desired effect or not, but they were at least listening attentively.

Vide turned to his daughter. "And shame on you, Maja. How dare you treat your brother and his wife the way you did?"

"But, *Far*, he's bewitched. The *duivel* can travel great distances with her thoughts. Arvid saw it with his own eyes." Maja's eyes seemed ready to pop out of their sockets. She pointed toward the big man who had not said a single word throughout the whole conversation. "Tell him, Arvid. Tell him what you saw."

"Quiet down, child!" Vide's voice was harsh, his eyes hot with anger. "Your brother told you a goddess gave her that gift. Why won't you believe your own brother?"

"Because he's under her spell." Jaali's sister whined like a small child, her lips contorting into a caricature of a frown. In spite of his anger, Jaali felt a twinge of pity for her—a child who was as much a victim of the kidnappings as he was. "He believes everything the *häxa* tells him. Someone had to stand up for him, to protect him."

The crowd was beginning to grumble again, emboldened by Maja's rebellion. They too did not believe in Milenda's innocence. The roar of agitated voices grew until it was impossible to tell one voice apart from the next.

"Stop!" A female voice echoed throughout the room, effectively silencing everyone. Jaali couldn't tell who had spoken, but a collective intake of breath pointed at someone not from this world.

A gust of unnatural wind swept everything for a moment. Standing by the door, almost naked and holding on to two forest cats on a leash, was Freya. The cats were almost as big as goats, with pointy ears and a luxuriant coat of hair, one golden, the other chocolate brown. She had obviously dressed to impress the villagers, and she had accomplished her mission—almost everyone in the room had their mouths open in awe of the spectacularly beautiful demigoddess.

"I was hoping not to have to interfere," she began, her mouth twitching in disgust. "But it looks like my own children have become disobedient and disrespectful of their gods. In how many ways do I need to tell you to leave Milenda and Jaali be? Do I have to smite you to get you to listen to me? Because I can do that." The goddess looked formidable, and Jaali would bet there wasn't a single soul in there willing to go against her just then.

Freya strutted around the small space, stopping once in a while to scan a young male from top to bottom in that disturbingly lascivious way that made Jaali shiver.

"I'm only going to say this once." Every eye was glued to her, following her every move, a crazed glare that betrayed their fear. "Let my two protégées live their life in peace. No more talk of witchcraft and *duivels*. Milenda has been chosen by the gods to change things in her nation. Things that affect you more than anybody else. So leave her be."

Jaali watched half amused as the villagers nodded their heads in unison. Only his father retained a look of serenity.

"Milenda is with child." There was a loud intake of breath and a murmur of voices. "You will allow her to deliver and nurture this baby in safety and comfort until she must return to her nation and claim her heritage. If you do not, I'll be obliged to interfere again. And then, I promise, I will not be half as nice."

The goddess turned her back, pulling on the restrains of her cats, and headed for the exit. But before she vanished—

for Jaali knew she had no intention of using something as mundane as the door—she turned around one last time.

"Almost forgot. If you as much as lift a finger to harm my beautiful wyverns, I will indeed bring Thor's hammer down on you." With that, she wavered like a mirage and vanished in a dramatic poof of smoke.

NEW BEGINNINGS

Milenda

Milenda laughed, her giggles competing with the chirping of birds outside the window. "That tickles, Jaali." It was a half-hearted complaint. As much as it did tickle, the fluttery of her husband's lips over her swollen belly was welcomed. His kiss always brought soothing and healing to her body and soul.

Jaali continued to trail kisses up to her breasts, neck, and finally settled on her mouth, stretching his tall body along hers. "You taste even better now that you're pregnant."

She lifted her head quickly and surprised him with a stolen kiss. "Flatterer. I'm fat and ugly, and the only reason I taste good is because I've been bathing with those herbs Ebba gave me."

Ebba swore Milenda was about five months into her pregnancy, but the princess was not so sure. How could she tell? Even though Ebba seemed to have a knack for medicine, Milenda sometimes wished Mama Nyeusi was around. She had not been present when she was little—at least, not that she could remember—but she had heard the other servants talk about how she had been there when she was born. The old woman had been her mother's *iyalorixá* before her, and her midwife as well. Lately, Milenda found herself thinking about and yearning for those she left behind. She even missed Asha, her young servant girl who had been loyal and supportive.

And she missed her father. This, more than anything else, came as a shock considering their relationship had been almost nonexistent until close to her flight from Natale. But something had changed those last few weeks before her wedding, and the father-daughter connection that had been missing her whole life was suddenly and unexpectedly a reality. She so wished to nurture and see it grow.

Maybe it was her hormones making her wistful and brooding. Or maybe it was the distance. Life had finally settled into a peaceful routine. Perhaps the fact she didn't have to worry about being chased down and killed at every turn had opened the flood doors to wandering thoughts. They were happy now. Milenda had come down from the mountain shortly after her father-in-law's return, with Mjusi in tow, and they had quickly and easily settled down in their little house in the valley.

The snow was long gone, and a luxuriant green mantel stretched as far as the eye could see, interrupted here and there by trees. The river, now freed from the weight and restriction of ice, ran freely through the flat ground of *Hoppas.* The settlement had earned a new inhabitant. Ebba had been granted the right to live in one of the other abandoned houses in the valley and was now a mere walk away. Milenda liked having her close, especially when anxieties about the baby crawled into her chest and settled there. Her friend always seemed to have the right herb or the right words to put her fears to rest.

"What are you talking about, *msichana*?" Jaali's eyes followed his hand down to her belly and rested there, the warmth of his palm seeping pleasantly through her stretched-out skin into the life she carried within. "You're more beautiful than ever. You're carrying my child." His smile lit up the room. She had to laugh, treasuring the fact her husband was so much in love with the idea of having a baby.

"Good thing I'm heavy too, or I may just float away like a balloon." Her playful words held no truth at all. She was just as enamored by her pregnancy as Jaali seemed to be. Instead of worrying about losing her youthful looks, she cherished the swelling of her belly, choosing often to slide down her *kanga* skirt below it and allow the warm rays of the sun to caress her skin. It was a wondrous thing to know she was carrying a live being inside of her.

Supporting his head on his bent arm, Jaali twisted his nose and yawned. "As much as I'd love to lie here with you, I promised my father I would meet him down at the river for fishing." He planted a kiss on her nose and rolled off the bed. "Do you want to come?"

Milenda rubbed her underbelly and shook her head.

She wanted Jaali to have as much time with his father as he could. Eventually, they would have to return to Natale, and the gods only knew when he'd be able to see his father again. "No, you go by yourself. I have a date myself."

Jaali shot a glance at her, his eyes narrowing under a wrinkled brow. "A date? With whom? Do I have to remind you you're a married woman?"

Milenda laughed. Her date was with the wyverns that had taken to visiting her a few times a week. The whole family would fly down the side of the mountain and visit the valley for a while. Milenda loved their company, and so did Mjusi, who insisted on staying with her rather than his new family.

She slid off the bed and began toward the bathroom. Her bladder didn't like laughter too much lately. "See what you did? Now I have to go." She skipped on bare feet across the room, and yelled out, "Might as well take a shower."

In the last couple months, Jaali had finished building her the promised shower. It was not like the ones in the palace, of course, but it was lovely and practical. Now that the river ran free again, they had plenty of water, and she indulged in long showers every morning. More often than not in her husband's company.

She felt him before she saw him, his body molding itself against her bare back, the cool water pouring and running down both their bodies. "I thought you needed to leave," Milenda said, a sigh of pleasure escaping her lips as Jaali's hardness rubbed against her skin. His arms had come around and crossed against her breasts.

"My father will wait a bit longer." His whisper, blown into her ear, made her shiver.

Milenda caressed his arm, her fingers tracing the visible edge of his tattoo—a new addition to his scarred and yet perfect body. It matched hers to symbolize their union. Ebba had told the princess about her people's tradition of matching tattoos as a wedding symbol, and Milenda had not wasted any time convincing her husband they should get one. "That way it will be obvious to anyone that we are indeed married." He had laughed but agreed to do it. The tattoos were on the back of their right forearms, a stylized picture of a *mitzu* stretching from the wrist up almost to the bend of the elbow. It was simple and beautiful.

Jaali's hands slid down to brush over her belly in a circular motion that started at the top of the swell and curved all the way down under it. She moaned, a tiny sound that carried the overwhelming mix of feelings her northern man always stirred up. She turned around to face him. Their wet bodies, glued together by desire, shivered against each other—not from the chill of the water, but from the heat their touch produced.

Milenda tilted her chin up to look into the endless pools of his eyes, and he brought his mouth down on hers, his tongue darting along the seam of her lips before meeting hers in an exhilarating dance.

"Love you, *msichana*." Jaali placed his hands on her hips and moved as if to pick her up. "What...?" Pulling slightly apart from her, Jaali looked her in the eye, a question furrowing his brow. "What was that?"

Milenda's *matangazos* were ablaze. Her smile stretched to impossible widths, and she pulled herself tighter against Jaali. They both felt it then, the flurry of movement, like a miniature wave made of flesh and bone, or the fluttering wings of a butterfly against their bodies. "It's Johari, our daughter." She pressed her swollen belly harder against him, and the baby obliged with another soft movement.

Jaali's face had blanched, and his breath became shallow. He stood still, his naked body pressed against his wife's, their child dancing for the both of them. "Daughter?" His voice was but a squeak.

"Yes, you fool. Your child. You know, the one I'm carrying." Milenda laughed at the shocked expression on his face. His already ivory complexion had gone even whiter. "Are you all right?"

It took him a few seconds, but eventually color came back to his cheeks and the smile back to his lips. "Johari, is it? And how can you be so sure it's a girl? Has it spoken to you?"

Milenda nodded. She knew he was joking, but he was not too far from the truth. Her gift apparently had other benefits. "I'm as connected to her as I am to you, *wimbo wa moyo*. It's a girl."

With the baby still dancing around between them, Jaali bent down and kissed his wife. "Why Johari?"

"Johari because she is precious to us, and Joka because she will have the soul and courage of a *msitu*, a dragon." What she didn't say was that their daughter would have to be strong just like her mother. Being a royal heir was not a walk in the park.

Reaching behind her, Jaali turned off the water and grabbed the towel that hung from a peg on the wall. Unwilling to sever their contact, he draped the large towel around both of them and stood still for a while longer, cherishing the heat their two bodies produced and in awe of the life they had created together.

"Johari Joka Asker, kind of a mouthful, but I like it."

A scratching noise from just outside the bathroom told them Mjusi was not happy with the wait. "I better go," Milenda said, chuckling softly. "He misses his family already."

They both dressed and left, Jaali in the direction of town and Milenda toward the edge of the forest. Mjusi was beside her, half flying, half walking. It didn't take long before they saw the dark silhouettes of the wyverns in the distance— two large and two smaller ones, the span of their wings stretching farther than seemed possible as they glided down from the side of the mountain into the valley below.

Milenda could now tell the subtle differences between the wyverns. The family, while obviously the same species as Mjusi, had characteristics that were common to the four of them but not the *msitu*. Their eyes were all the color of amber, almost the same color as Milenda's skin, and their scales, while of different colors, were all the same shape. Her childhood friend had dark, forest green eyes, and his scales were longer and narrower than those of the other wyverns.

Mjusi took off flying to meet them, huffing and puffing

in that funny way of his, and Milenda watched the smaller ones as they sidled next to him, playfully nudging him with their snouts. She wondered if there were more of them in these mountains or if these were the last of their species. What would happen when she went back to Natale? Would Mjusi stay behind with his new family or would he want to go back with her?

She noticed Mama Msitu carrying something hanging from her powerful jaws. Was she bringing Milenda food out of habit? After all, she had kept the princess fed throughout her time in the wyverns's lair, pretty much the same way she had fed her own fledglings. As she approached, she noticed that whatever she was carrying was moving. Milenda automatically cringed, remembering the time Mjusi had brought her a bloodied desert rodent as a gift.

When they were just a few feet apart, the female wyvern gently dropped her cargo into the soft grass and nuzzled it in a gesture that strangely mimicked a caress. Melinda rushed forward to see what it was.

Lying under the protection of Mama Msitu's long, scaly neck was a tiny wyvern, too young to stand on its own. Milenda cautiously kneeled down by it and brushed her hand over the still-soft scales of the creature.

"It's a baby." It had never occurred to her that the dragon was pregnant, or that there were eggs somewhere. How did wyverns have babies anyway? Milenda realized she still knew so little about these amazing creatures. "Is it yours?"

The powerful female shook her head from side to side in an undeniable negative. This was not her own fledgling.

Then, where had this baby come from?

Mjusi had scooted closer and began tapping the fledgling gently with his head and making clicking sounds the princess now recognized as sounds of endearment of some kind. "You like it, Mjusi? Is it a girl or a boy?" The young animal cooed and closed his big green eyes in delight. "It looks like you. Same coloring."

The small creature's narrow scales mirrored those of her childhood friend as well. Could this creature be closely related to her *msitu*? And if so, why had the wyverns brought it to her in the valley? Not for the first time, she wished she could talk to them.

The little ones scampered around, chasing each other and occasionally taking off in short but dizzying flights while the older ones seemed content just lying in the warm sun watching the young ones playing. Milenda sat on the grass near the baby that had cuddled against her legs and fallen asleep. Could the creature tell she was with child and her motherly instincts were kicking in?

When the sun began setting slowly in the horizon, the adult dragons called their charges and prepared to leave. Milenda was still holding the little one on her lap. "Wait! Aren't you forgetting the baby?"

Mama Msitu turned to her and roared, throwing her head backward and then shaking it a few times. She was not going to take the baby back. With the usual gale of dust and leaves, the four wyverns took flight, leaving her and Mjusi in charge of the baby. What was she going to do with a fledgling?

Even though still tiny, the creature already weighed more than a small human toddler, and Milenda had to rest several times on her way to the house. Jaali was waiting for her, sitting on the grass, his back against the front wall of their house. He jumped to his feet when he realized she was carrying something heavy and ran to her aid.

"A dragon?"

Milenda laughed at the look of surprise on his face and handed him the small creature. "Long story. I'll tell you after I drink something cold."

The night was pushing the daylight behind the horizon. By the time Milenda had explained the events of the day, Mjusi had curled up by the unlit hearth with his tail and muzzle protectively around the fledgling and fallen asleep. Lying in bed, Jaali cradled Milenda in his arms and whispered words in her ear, stories about the day fishing with his father and how it had made him feel.

"Do you two ever do anything else?" Freya waved her hand in their direction. "Don't you get tired of each other?"

Milenda looked up at the goddess and nearly choked on her own tongue. Freya was not alone. Beside her, a tall and slim figure of an Afrikan woman stood quiet and still.

"Yemanjá!" Milenda sat up, her jaw falling open at the sight of the demigoddess. She hadn't seen or heard from her since their journey there. "Mother, what are you doing here?" She couldn't help but feeling nervous. The goddess always seemed to appear right before some sort of epic news.

The dark woman smiled, and Milenda marveled at how

incredibly different the two goddesses, now standing side by side, really were. Yemanjá smile oozed love and sincerity while Freya's was often sarcastic and dripping in double entendres.

"My sweet Jewel, you look well." Jaali seemed frozen, half sitting up, half laying down. He had never seen the Afrikan goddess, and for a moment Milenda thought that maybe two goddesses at the same time was too much for him to handle. "You too, young Fjorden. I have been following your progress with much interest. Your love for my princess is unmatched. I am impressed and encouraged by its power."

Milenda watched, with some amusement, as Jaali gulped, his Adam's apple bobbing up and down on his throat, liquid eyes still bulging slightly.

"What do we owe the pleasure of your visit, Mother?" The princess fell into the more formal speech, remembering Mama Nyeusi's words of caution. *You must always speak to deities with due deference, my child.*

"My sister, Freya, brought me the good news." Yemanjá glanced toward the other goddess who was glaring at Jaali, still too stunned to speak. "I'm so very happy for you. Soon, you'll be able to go back and claim your right to the throne of Natale."

Jaali found his voice. "Not before the baby's born, surely." He looked outraged as he swung his legs over the edge of the bed and sat next to his wife.

Yemanjá laughed softly, her many gold bangles jingling as she waved a hand in front of her. "Of course not. We must let this baby grow strong before making the journey back." Her dark brown eyes bore into Milenda's. "Your father has not produced an heir yet. Your *iyalorixá* has been working her magic well." She covered her mouth as she laughed again. "You'll be the undisputed heir to the throne when you go back. And Jaali your consort."

Milenda shook her head, sending her loose hair flying against Jaali's face. "What makes you think the Elders will go down without a fight?"

The black goddess sobered up, and even Freya's sarcastic smile faded. "Who said anything about it being easy? They *will* fight, tooth and nail, to keep their power over the people—and the royalty—of Natale. You must win that fight."

Milenda's heart dropped. "But I'm not a warrior. I don't know how to fight. I know nothing about the politics of my country." Jaali slid an arm over her shoulders, pulling her gently against him. "How can I fight them?"

"Jewel, you're a Nyota, and you have gifts you don't even realize you have. When the time comes, you'll know what to do, just like you knew how to reach out to Jaali in the desert. No one taught you that. You just knew." Yemanjá took a few steps forward and touched her shoulder. The *matangazos* lit up and burned. "When the time comes, my Jewel, you will stand up and fight."

A whimper distracted them all. Mjusi fussed over the baby wyvern, caressing his back scales with a long-forked tongue. Milenda laughed in spite of her anxiety. The *msitu* was taking his responsibility over the fledgling seriously.

Freya laughed out loud. "Gåva, you're here." Milenda couldn't believe her eyes as the goddess ran to kneel next to the baby in obvious joy. The baby dragon opened its eyes and wagged his tail like a puppy. "So they brought you little Gåva already. Good, obedient wyverns."

Yemanjá smiled at the little creature who rolled onto its back and was now delighting in the belly rubs Freya was bestowing upon him. "Who's this funny creature, my sister?"

The almost naked goddess kissed Gåva's snout and stood. "A gift for Mjusi. A little female company he can take back to Natale and build a family with."

Was Freya playing matchmaker with the dragons? "It looks like Mjusi," Milenda said. "Are they related?"

Freya nodded. "Same line of wyverns, yes. Gåva's a very distant cousin. She's also an orphan in need of care. Her parents died a couple weeks ago on the other side of the mountains, and your wyverns have been taking care of her since then."

"Gåva means gift." Jaali's voice surprised everyone, even the goddesses who stared at him. "Thank you. I'm sure Mjusi is very grateful for the company."

Milenda was surprised by Freya's generosity. The goddess had never seemed very aware of the needs or wants of others, but with this gift, she had done something not only extremely generous for Mjusi but also for Milenda's daughter.

"Thank you, Freya. Gåva will be a wonderful friend for our daughter, just like Mjusi was for me. Being a princess can be very lonely sometimes." Jaali squeezed her arm gently and smiled at her, his ocean-filled eyes glittering in the semidarkness. "It was very generous of you."

Freya let go of the baby wyvern and stood up, her translucent wrap skirt falling in folds and waves to her bare feet. "Just looking out for one of my creatures," she said, swiping her hair off her shoulders. "Wyverns have a special place in my heart."

"Children, we must go." It was Yemanjá, her *kanga*-covered body thin and long and just as tall as her northern sister. "I will see you again when it's time. Enjoy these days of peace, family, and warmth." Her words, so positive on the surface, had a dark undertone, a shadow of hard things to come. Milenda shivered against Jaali and watched as the two goddesses dissipated like smoke into the air.

Hearts filled with a mixture of joy and apprehension, the couple went outside into the night air and sat together by the door as they often did. The stars were glowing full force in the dark sky, and the temperature had dropped enough that Milenda's arms were covered in goose bumps. Jaali fetched their *nguba* inside the house before dropping beside her on the grassy patch by their front door. Mjusi and Gåva were fast asleep, molded against each other, a few steps away from where Jaali and Milenda snuggled under the blanket and watched the stars blink at the land beneath them.

"Will you miss it, *wimbo wa moyo*? When we leave." She'd be going home, but he would be saying goodbye to his own for the second time.

Jaali sighed. "I will, despite all our troubles, I think I will. I'll miss my father and Ebba. Our little house and the northern lights." He flattened his hand against Milenda's belly. "I'll miss our showers together." She giggled, her *matangazos* warming up and glowing. "But what matters the most, *msichana*, is that we stay together. Together we can face anything."

Milenda burrowed further against him, her hand on his chest, relishing the comfort of his heat, the song of his heartbeat. "True, we're a great team. But I can't help but fear the years ahead. When we go back to Natale, we'll be up against odds that do not favor us. We're up against something ancient and all-powerful—the Elders and their culture of fear and superstition. You saw what happened with your own people."

"Yemanjá was right about one thing, and you should heed her advice." Jaali kissed the top of her head that lay just underneath his chin. "We have this time, we have now. And now is very good. Instead of worrying about what may happen, we should focus on what is happening instead. We're together, we're about to become parents, my people have finally accepted you, and I'm getting to know my father again. We're so fortunate we have this now. Let's enjoy it while we can and worry about the future much later."

Milenda turned her face up to him and smiled. "You were always the smart one in this relationship," she said with a giggle. "I have the looks; you have the brains."

Jaali captured her lips and ran his tongue along the seam of hers. "Are you trying to tell me I'm ugly?" His teasing whisper caressed her skin as effectively as his fingers, and she trembled in his arms, happy and serene.

"I love you, *msichana*."

"I love you, *wimbo wa moyo*. And always will."

Folds and waves of color turned the skies into an artist canvas with splashes of lavender and blues. The couple stared in awe. It was the wrong time of the year for the amazing spectacle, and yet, there it was, a festival of light and color. Milenda couldn't shake the feeling it was a show being performed for them alone, a gift from the goddesses. They leaned onto each other, Milenda's head falling softly on Jaali's shoulder, and watched the miracle happening before their eyes. However frightening the future might be, Milenda knew their love was strong enough to weather it. And so did the goddesses, it seemed.

GLOSSARY

The Afrikan language used in this book is very loosely based on Swahili and other African dialects, while Jaali's native language is based on several northern European languages such as Dutch and Swedish. Here's a list of the terms used in the story and their translations.

borgmästare – mayor
bror – brother
duivel – devil
for søren – damn! holy crap!
fjorden – someone from the northern lands
gåva – gift
gemenskap hus – community center
genomdrivare – enforcer
gele – very elaborate head wrap that often reaches great heights
häxa – witch
hema – primitive home
indent – Natalian term for slave
iqhiya – headband, turban
isigolwani – decorative neck hoop

iyalorixá – priestess serving as a go-between for mortals and the orisas

johari – something of value, jewel,

joka – dragon

kanga – printed fabric, typical wrap dress (skirt or shirt)

kidogo moja – little one

kijani – green

liten älg – little elk

litet barn – little child

malaika – angel

matangazos – (noticeable) markings

Mjusi msitu – forest lizard

msichana – respectful term for girl

nasikitika – I'm sorry

nguba – wedding ceremonial blanket/wrap

odjur – beast

orisas – minor gods

seiðmenn – weaver of destiny

shetani – the devil

smutsigt tjuv – filthy thief

tack så mycket – thank you so much

theluji – snow

trevligt att träffas – a pleasure to meet you

vad vill du? – what do you want?

vänner – friends

vem är där – who's there?

wimbo wa moyo – heart's song

zambarau – purple

ACKNOWLEDGMENTS

The Jewel Chronicles series is very special to me because it allowed me to write across some of my favorite genres with the unusual flavor of Africa mixed in. *Snow Jewel* was a labor of love and I'm looking forward to writing the last in the series which will see the return of Princess Milenda and her consort to Afrika.

I want to thank all the readers who have encouraged me with their kind words and their enthusiasm throughout this journey. You are amazing!

My online writer friends who have cheered me on when I was discouraged, the great people of Writers' Soapbox and my sprinting partners, A.L. Vincent, Sara Schoen, and Marianne Rice. Thank you all so much for your feedback, pep talks, and company (however virtual).

My local critique group, The Writing Room, led by the talented Rob Solka (also known as the Super Librarian), who lifted me up with their kind words and helpful advice.

A heartfelt thank you to the Sippy Cups and Semantics. I'm so honored to be part of a group of such talented writers and amazing women.

P.A. Duncan, thank you so much for reading my manuscript and giving me such great feedback, especially about Nordic mythology. I can't tell you how much I appreciate it.

My family for supporting me in this crazy ride and putting up with my flights of fancy.

With endless admiration for all the women who, like Milenda, are willing to step up to the plate to make this a better world. Thank you for inspiring me with your courage and spunk.

Finally, a word of sincere gratitude to my publisher, Becky and my editors, Virginia Cantrell, Barbara Hoover, and Jenny Zepeda. You guys make this writing business look easy.

ABOUT THE AUTHOR

Natalina wrote her first romance in collaboration with her best friend at the age of thirteen. Since then she has ventured into other genres, but romance is first and foremost in almost everything she writes. Her novel, *We Will Always Have the Closet*, is her first published romance.

After earning a degree in tourism and foreign languages, she worked as a tourist guide in her native country, Portugal, for a short time before moving to the United States. She's lived in three continents and a few islands, and her knack for languages and linguistics led her to a master's degree in education. She lives in Virginia where she has taught English as a second language to elementary school children for more years than she cares to admit.

Natalina doesn't believe you can have too many books or too much coffee. Art and dance make her happy and she is pretty sure she could survive on lobster and bananas alone.

When she is not writing or stressing over lesson plans, she shares her life with her husband and two adult sons.

Facebook: www.facebook.com/Authornatalinareis

ABOUT THE PUBLISHER

Hot Tree Publishing opened its doors in 2015 with an aspiration to bring quality fiction to the world of readers. With the initial focus on romance and a wide spread of romance sub-genres, we envision opening up to alternative genres in the near future.

Firmly seated in the industry as a leading editing provider to independent authors and small publishing houses, Hot Tree Publishing is the sister company to Hot Tree Editing, founded in 2012. Having established in-house editing and promotions, plus having a well-respected market presence, Hot Tree Publishing endeavors to be a leader in bringing quality stories to the world of readers.

Interested in discovering more amazing reads brought to you by Hot Tree Publishing? Head over to the website for information:

WWW.HOTTREEPUBLISHING.COM